"Midas, you have pleased me greatly," Bacchus said. "To thank you, and to express my divine appreciation, I will grant you . . ."

The god paused dramatically and glanced back at his servants. One of them pulled a small drum from his robes and began a drumroll.

". . . one wish!" Bacchus finished.

"A wish?" Midas cocked his ears. "You mean anything?"

Bacchus nodded. "Anything."

"Oh, wow! Oh, wow!" Midas was so excited, he jumped up and did a flip in the air. "This is so great! Let me think. I've already got a wonderful wife, a darling daughter, and a happy kingdom. What should I wish for?"

Ideas dog-paddled around and around Midas's head. Fame? Fortune? A lifetime supply of big, juicy steaks?

Suddenly, Midas thought of something that would make him richer than anyone on earth. "I've got it!" he announced. "I wish—"

"Take your time," Bacchus interrupted. "Think about it carefully."

But Midas ignored his warning. "I wish for the golden touch!"

WISHBONE ADVENTURES

Curse of Gold

BIG RED CHAIR BOOKS™

A Division of Lyrick Publishing™

WISHBONE™
created by Rick Duffield

This book is a work of fiction. The characters, incidents, and dialogues are products of the author's imagination and are not to be construed as real. Any resemblance to actual events or persons, living or dead, is entirely coincidental.

Big Red Chair Books™, A Division of Lyrick Publishing™
300 E. Bethany Drive, Allen, Texas 75002

Produced by By George Productions, Inc.
Interior Illustrations by Steven Petruccio

Library of Congress Catalog Card Number: 00-103256
ISBN: 1-57064-432-2

First printing: July 2000
Printed in the United States of America
10 9 8 7 6 5 4 3 2

DEDICATION

In memory of Ovid for his timeless work, *Metamorphoses*. The author also thanks Joanne Mattern for her help in preparing this manuscript.

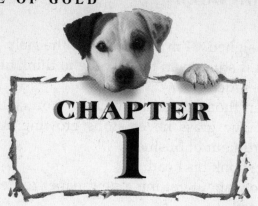

CHAPTER 1

Wishbone sat on the front porch of the Talbots' house. His small black nose twitched in the warm spring breeze. His tail wagged happily. It was a beautiful, sunny Saturday, and the little Jack Russell terrier was ready for adventure.

"Come on, Joe," Wishbone said impatiently. "It's too nice just to sit here. Let's go for a walk!"

Beside him, Wishbone's best friend, Joe Talbot, was reading the newspaper. His normally happy face was scrunched into a frown.

"Helllooo! Joe? Why are we just sitting here on such a nice day?" Wishbone tried again.

Just then, Joe's mother, Ellen, walked over with the mail. Ellen had brown hair and a bright smile just like her son's. She was also in charge of all meals, snacks, and treats in the Talbot household. That was a very important job as far as Wishbone was concerned.

Ellen sat down on the porch. "What are you doing, Joe?"

Joe sighed. "I'm checking out the Help Wanted section. I still haven't been able to think of a good business idea."

Ellen thought for a moment. "You could mow lawns. The grass never stops growing, so you'd never run out of business."

Joe shook his head.

"How about getting a newspaper route?" Ellen suggested.

"No, I want to start a real business and make real money. Remember that kid we saw on the news? He started a discount computer business on the Internet. He gets orders from all over the country for thousands of dollars. I could do something like that."

"Hey, Joe, I've got a great idea." Wishbone lay down and rolled onto his back. "Why not start a stomach-rubbing business? There's a huge demand right down here."

"Joe, I know a business like that sounds exciting. But do you realize how much work it is to run your own business?" Ellen asked. "Your life would be completely different. I don't know if it's worth the trade-offs you'd have to make. Anyway, you're only twelve. There's more than enough time to work for money when you're grown up. Right now, you should concentrate on school and having fun with your friends."

"Yeah, Joe," Wishbone agreed. "You're young. Enjoy life! Read a book! Chew on a

bone! Drink out of the toilet! Okay, that last

one was a joke," he added quickly.

"But Mom—" Joe was interrupted by a loud screech from next door.

Wishbone dove for cover, ducking his head under his paws. "What in the world was that?" Cautiously, he lifted his head to look.

Wanda Gilmore, the Talbots' next-door neighbor, sped into her driveway. Her old white convertible stopped with a lurch and a squeal of the brakes. Wishbone covered his ears. "Hey, watch it! Those high-pitched noises are tough on these little ears," he complained.

Wishbone watched as Wanda leaped out of her car. Then the tall, thin woman with short dark hair rushed around to the trunk. The brim of her oversized purple hat bounced up and down. A green-and-orange-striped scarf trailed behind her.

Wanda jerked open the trunk of her car. She yanked out a bulging bag of groceries. Then she wrenched out another, and another, and another.

Wow, Wanda sure must be hungry, the little dog thought. *I'd like to get my paws on all those bags!*

Wanda staggered up her front walk. She had two grocery bags balanced on one arm and three more on the other. She held another bag between her clenched teeth.

"Hi, Miss Gilmore," Joe called from the porch. "Did you think of any good business ideas for me?"

"Mmmff!" Wanda cried. She shook her head. Her hat slid down over her eyes, knocking her oversized, pink-rimmed sunglasses down her nose.

Joe looked concerned. "Hey, do you want some help?" he asked.

"Yes!" Wanda cried. But as soon as she opened her mouth, the bag slipped out. She lunged forward to grab it. The other bags began to slide.

"Look out! Avalanche!" Wishbone cried. He ducked behind Joe as the bags tumbled out of Wanda's arms.

Wanda gazed sadly at her groceries, which were now scattered all over the walkway. "Yes, I could use a hand," she finished with a sigh.

Ellen hurried forward. "Oh, Wanda, I'm sorry! Joe and I just weren't thinking. We shouldn't have just sat there when you needed help."

Joe and Ellen knelt down to help Wanda clean up. Wishbone sniffed at the spilled groceries. He nosed a can of soup toward Joe. "Here you go." He wagged his tail hopefully. "Hey, does anyone have a can opener?"

Wanda looked down at the eggs in several open cartons. She held up a goopy eggshell. Yolk dribbled from her fingers.

"If we can put a man on the moon, why can't we make a better eggshell?" Wanda demanded. She began putting her spilled groceries back into the bags. "I have to bake four angel food cakes for the Historical Society. Then I have to teach drawing at the Senior Center at six o'clock. And I have to type up the newsletter for the Arbor Society by tomorrow." Her voice rose into a wail. "How am I ever going to find an extra forty minutes to go shopping again?"

"I'll go, Miss Gilmore," Joe volunteered.

"Oh, would you?" Wanda's big eyes widened. She smiled gratefully. "You're a lifesaver, Joe."

Wishbone licked at another egg carton full of broken eggs. "I'll clean this up," he said around a mouthful of egg. "Don't bother to thank me, Wanda. It's my pleasure. Really!"

Later that afternoon, Wishbone lay on the floor in Wanda's kitchen. Joe sat at the kitchen table. He was helping Wanda make her cakes for the Historical Society.

Nearby, Wanda sat in front of her enormous

pottery wheel. Flour was smeared on her face. As she talked to Joe, she used one foot to spin the wheel at its base. A bowl of cake batter sat on top of the wheel. As the bowl spun, Wanda mixed the batter. "Yes, sirree," Wanda finished. "That's when I thought, 'This is it! This is how Joe's going to bring home the bacon!'"

Wishbone lifted his head and cocked his ears. "Did somebody say bacon?"

Joe cracked an egg and carefully separated the white from the yolk. He looked confused. "By separating eggs?"

"No, by delivering them," Wanda explained. "I know I'm not the only one who's too busy or tired to go grocery shopping." She grinned at Joe. "How does ten dollars a delivery sound?"

Joe's eyes lit up. "That's great! That's really great! I've been trying so hard to think of a good business idea."

"I know," Wanda said enthusiastically. "Believe me, if you want it, you'll have more business than you can handle. I'll tell everyone! There's my gardening group, my drawing students at the Senior Center, the Historical Society . . ."

"A business! My very own business!" Joe's eyes were shining.

"A career in food!" Wishbone said. "That's an excellent idea. I can't believe I didn't think of it myself."

 Wow, Joe is as excited as a dog with a new bone. Well, there's nothing like an exciting opportunity to start your heart pounding and your tail wagging.

This reminds me of another guy who thought he'd found the opportunity of a lifetime. It's the ancient Greek myth of King Midas. Midas's story was told by Ovid, a poet in ancient Rome. Ovid wrote about it in his most famous poem, *Metamorphoses*. "Metamorphoses" means "transformations" or "changes." And Midas sure did go through some pretty amazing changes!

CHAPTER 2

Wishbone closed his eyes and imagined himself as Midas. He pictured a palace filled with marble columns. Rose bushes and olive trees filled the courtyards. The palace was in the city of Gordion, the capital of the kingdom of Phrygia.

King Midas sat in a room that faced an open courtyard. The king's chair was made of carved wood with a woven leather seat and soft silk cushions.

Warm breezes from the Aegean Sea wafted through the palace courtyard. The breeze ruffled the fur on the king's back. Midas gnawed on a lamb bone left over from lunch.

Ah, the taste of lamb in my mouth. The scent of roses in my nose! Midas thought happily. He heard the laughter of his young daughter, Ariel, coming from outside. His tail wagged. Life was good.

Midas stopped chewing and sniffed the air. He sensed someone was approaching.

A servant dressed in a simple robe entered the chamber. His eyes were wide.

"Yes, what is it?" Midas asked. *This had better be important,* he thought. *I hate being interrupted in the middle of a good chew.*

The servant bowed to the king. "Your Highness, you have a visitor." Midas could smell the man's excitement and nervousness.

"Who is it?" Midas asked. "You're acting as if the gods themselves have come to call."

The servant nodded. "They have! I mean, one of them has, Your Highness. It is Pan who wishes to see you."

Midas shook his ears. Had he heard correctly? "Pan?" he repeated. He jumped onto all four paws. "You mean, the god Pan? Pan, the god of woods and shepherds?"

The servant nodded again.

Now the king, too, was trembling with excitement from

> **What does Midas mean when he talks about Pan being "the god of woods and shepherds"? The ancient Greeks believed every place, person, thing, or occupation had a god attached to it. That god had a special connection to the person or place and often helped people who were connected to it. Check out my handy list of the Greek gods and goddesses at the end of this chapter.**

9

his nose to the tip of his tail. *Just think, a genuine god here to see me! Nothing like this has ever happened to me before!* He quickly shoved his lamb bone under a cushion. "Well, what are you waiting for? Show him in!"

Midas hopped down from his chair. He began running in excited circles on the floor.

The servant hurried away. A few moments later, Pan entered the chamber. Midas stared at him in awe. The god was twice the size of an ordinary mortal. From the waist up, he looked like a man. But he had hairy legs and hooves like a goat. A wreath of olive leaves crowned the god's dark curls. He held a bunch of wild berries in one hand. Tucked under his other arm was a wooden flute.

Midas bowed his head all the way down to his front paws. "Welcome to Phrygia, O immortal one."

"Yeah, thanks," Pan answered, yawning. He popped a berry into his mouth. "Charming little kingdom you have here, King . . . uh, King . . ."

"Midas," the king supplied. His tail wagged eagerly. "I am King Midas of Phrygia."

"Oh, right," Pan said with a shrug. "Well, King Midas of Phrygia, I'm here to ask you to do a little job for me."

"Certainly." Midas sat at complete attention. This could be important. Not to mention that Pan might accidentally drop one of those berries onto the floor.

"I need you to help me settle something," Pan explained. He grinned at Midas, his green eyes sparkling. "Somebody has issued me a little challenge."

Midas could hardly believe his ears. "Who would be so foolish as to challenge a god?" he wondered out loud.

Pan burst into laughter. "Good point." He strolled across the floor and sat down in Midas's own chair. The god tucked his enormous goat legs under his body.

Midas waited, his head cocked to one side.

"Anyway, this foolish challenger has suggested a music contest." Pan put his flute to his lips. He piped out a complicated series of notes at dazzling speed. Then he grinned. "I'm sure you know that I play the flute. Shepherd tunes are my specialty."

"Yes, of course," Midas answered.

Pan tucked his flute back under his arm. He tossed a berry in the air and caught it in his mouth. "I met this other fellow in the woods not far from here. He boasted that he was a better musician. So we decided to have a competition to settle the matter. And"—he pointed his flute at the king—"you, Midas, will be the judge."

Midas's chest swelled with pride. "I would be most honored to judge the contest, O immortal one." By next week, he thought, everyone in the empire will be talking about this. He was so excited, he leaped into the air and did a little flip.

"I'm glad to see that you're so enthusiastic, Midas." Pan's eyes danced mischievously. "There's just one thing, though. A minor detail, really."

"Anything," Midas agreed happily. "You name it, you got it."

Pan sat up straight. He leaned forward over his long goat legs to look straight into Midas's eyes.

"It's the little question of how you're going to judge the contest," Pan said.

Midas cocked his ears. "I'm not sure I know what you mean."

Pan stood up. He towered over the king.

Midas felt a shiver of fear run down his spine. His ears flattened against his skull.

Pan leaned down toward Midas. "You realize that we're talking about my reputation here," he said in a quiet, reasonable voice. "It would be most

12

embarrassing if I didn't win this little contest." His gleaming green eyes locked onto the king's brown ones. "But I'm sure I don't have to worry about you making the right choice. I can tell you know how to be loyal to a friend."

"Oh, I get it," Midas said, nodding slowly. "You want me to name you the winner." He scratched at his ear with his back paw. "Actually, I had planned on listening to the music first. After all, how could I make a decision without—wait a minute." Midas sat up straight. "Did you say I was your friend?"

"I know we only just met," Pan said with a sly smile. "But somehow I have the feeling I can count on you. Why, I think of you as a friend already. A good friend."

"Sure, me too," Midas said eagerly. He raised his head proudly. *King Midas of Phrygia, friend of the gods. I like the sound of that.* Thoughts began dog-paddling around in his head. He saw Pan introducing him to the other gods, who quickly became his buddies as well. He imagined Pan coming over for dinner and sharing stories around the table with Midas and his friends. Hey, maybe Pan could even get him VIP seats for the next Olympic Games!

The Olympic Games were invented by the ancient Greeks sometime before 900 B.C. They developed from ceremonies held to honor the gods. By 776 B.C., the games became a regular event. They were held every four years.

Those long-ago Olympics were very different from the ones we have today. There were only a few events, including races, the pentathlon (one competition that involved five events: running, jumping, throwing the discus, throwing the javelin, and wrestling), and a rough combination of boxing and wrestling that was called pankration. There were no women athletes in the early Olympics—only men were allowed to compete. In fact, women and slaves weren't even allowed to watch the games!

As the years went by, the Olympics became corrupt. Christians also objected to honoring so many gods and goddesses. Finally, in A.D. 393, the Christian Emperor Theodosius I banned the Olympic Games altogether. The games disappeared for more than 1,500 years, until athletes and European officials decided to start having the games again in 1896.

Another difference was the length of the games. Until 692 B.C., the Olympics only lasted one day—not two weeks, as they do today! The Olympic champions didn't get flashy gold, silver, or bronze medals, either. They just received a crown of wild olive leaves, called a laurel. But those winners also received a lot of honor and fame.

Pan's voice broke into Midas's daydreams.

"So, do we have an understanding about the contest?" the god asked.

"Oh, absolutely. No problem, Pan," Midas replied. "You're a god, right? Who could be a better musician than you? Of course you'll win the contest."

"Wonderful! I thought you'd see it that way." Pan waved an arm in the air. There was a puff of green smoke. "I'm sure you won't mind if we seal our little agreement in writing then." A clay tablet magically appeared in Pan's hand. "Now, if you'll just sign this, please."

"Sign? Sure. Just let me read it first." Midas put his nose close to the densely written tablet.

"There's no need to bore yourself with the fine print. That comes into play only if you don't do what you promised. And you will, won't you?"

"Of course," Midas answered quickly.

"Then just make your mark on the dotted line," Pan said impatiently. "I haven't got all day, you know."

"Okay, sure thing." Midas pressed his paw into the still-soft clay. After all, what have I got to lose? he asked himself. Pan and I are pals now.

"There you go, Pan, old friend," Midas said. "Signed, sealed, and delivered."

15

WISHBONE'S GUIDE TO
THE GODS AND GODDESSES

Are you wondering what the deal is with all these gods? Why were they important?

Well, the ancient Greeks believed that the whole world was controlled by gods and goddesses. All the gods lived at the top of Mount Olympus, the highest mountain in Greece. They spent their time drinking nectar and eating ambrosia. Those were incredible-tasting foods that were supposed to make the gods live forever.

Unfortunately, hanging around and eating good food got pretty boring after a while. So the gods entertained themselves by playing around with human beings, teasing them, granting their wishes, punishing them for things the gods didn't like—stuff like that. Midas discovered firsthand what it was like to be the gods' plaything!

Here are some of the more important gods and goddesses:

ZEUS: The top dog in Godville (Mount Olympus). You definitely didn't want to make him angry, because he could do some major damage. The guy had a bad habit of throwing thunderbolts when he was upset. That could really singe your fur!

HERA: Zeus's wife, the queen of the gods. Hera had a pretty flashy temper, too! Get on her bad side or she might turn you into a cow—or worse.

ATHENA: The goddess of war and wisdom. One day, Zeus had a terrible headache. Then Athena popped out of his head, full-grown and dressed in battle gear. I guess Athena didn't have much of a childhood!

Along with being a warrior, Athena was a pretty bright girl. She invented the bridle, the trumpet, the flute, the pot, the rake, the plow, the yoke, the ship, and the chariot. Where would those Greeks be without her?

APOLLO: This guy had a blazing golden chariot that carried the sun across the sky every day. He was like the sled dog of the sky. Apollo was also the god of music. He could play a pretty mean lyre.

HADES: Not a happy guy, and no wonder. He was the lord of the underworld and had to hang out with dead people all the time.

ARTEMIS: She was the goddess of hunting and wild animals and also Apollo's twin sister. Artemis spent most of her time shooting arrows. And let me tell you, her aim was pretty impressive! She was also the goddess of childbirth, which might seem weird since she never had children. But she caused her mother no pain when she was born, so the Greeks named her the winner in the childbirth goddess category. Hey, it makes sense to me!

ARES: Nobody liked this guy. Even Hera and Zeus, his mom and dad, couldn't stand him. He was the god of war, and he had a lot of blood on his hands. But he was also considered a coward.

ERIS: Another unpopular goddess, Eris was Ares's sister. (Note their similar names.) Eris's idea of a good time was to cause trouble and get people mad at each other. That's why she was known as the goddess of discord. Because nobody liked her, Eris was often left off the guest list by both gods and humans. This was a bad idea; the Trojan War was a result of Eris not being invited to a wedding. But that's another story.

APHRODITE: The goddess of beauty and love. She never had any trouble getting a date, thanks to an odd item of clothing known as a girdle. Aphrodite's girdle was magic, and it forced anyone she wanted to fall in love with her.

HEPHAESTUS: This is the guy Aphrodite finally settled down with. Some people might think Hephaestus was an odd choice because he was . . . hey, there's no way to say this nicely . . . really ugly! In fact, Hera was so upset when she gave birth to an ugly child that she threw

Hephaestus into the sea and broke both of his legs. Thanks to that bit of motherly love, Hephaestus was lame. Anyway, Hephaestus was a blacksmith and made armor for all the gods. He used a volcano for a forge. Talk about fire power!

EROS: This guy was Aphrodite's son. Ever heard the saying "Love hurts"? Well, this little winged guy flew around shooting magic arrows at people to make them fall in love with each other. Ouch!

DEMETER: Demeter was the goddess of corn, grain, and the harvest. Without her help, the crops wouldn't grow, so the Greeks thought she was pretty cool. They even honored her by sacrificing the first loaf of bread from the harvest to her. I think that's a waste of good food, but what do I know?

The Greeks also believed that an unhappy incident in Demeter's life caused the four seasons. Demeter's daughter, Persephone, was kidnapped by Hades (you remember, that grumpy god of the underworld) to be his wife. Obviously, Demeter wasn't too thrilled about her new son-in-law. So she and Hades made a deal that Persephone would spend half the year in the land of the dead with Hades, and half the year on Mount Olympus with Mom. During the time that Persephone was in Hades, Demeter was too upset to allow crops to grow. So that's why we have winter. When Persephone comes back, it's spring!

PAN: Pan wasn't great-looking—how handsome could a guy with goat horns and goat feet be? But this god was lots of fun to have at parties. That's because Pan was an excellent musician, especially when it came to playing the flute. Unfortunately, Pan's musical talent would cause a lot of trouble for King Midas! Anyway, Pan was always running around in the woods, playing music and dancing. He made so much noise in the middle of the night that travelers often got scared. That's where the word "panic" comes from. Pan . . . panic . . . get it?

THE FATES: These three charming ladies were so old, they were around even before the gods. The Fates had incredible power, because they could determine how long a person lived, and whether that life would be good or evil.

Each Fate had a specific job. Clothos was the spinner who spun the thread of life. Lachesis was the measurer. She got to choose what the life would be like and how long it would be. Atropos was the scariest, because she ran around with a big pair of scissors and cut the thread of life when it was a person's time to die.

POSEIDON: God of the ocean. This was the guy to blame if your fishing boat sank or a tidal wave wiped out your village.

BACCHUS: A total party animal. This god never missed a good time. He was the former student of a man named Silenus, whom Midas would help out of a bad situation.

CHAPTER
3

The moment Midas pressed his paw into the clay tablet, Pan clapped his hands. In a puff of green smoke, the room filled with the most important nobles of Phrygia.

"Hey, great trick!" Midas trotted eagerly around the room. "Welcome! Glad you could make it on such short notice. You're in for a real treat today. Have you met my friend, Pan?" His tail wagged proudly.

Midas grabbed a passing servant. "Bring food and drinks right away. And fetch my wife and daughter," he ordered. *I don't want my family to miss my finest hour*, he thought.

A few moments later, Midas's wife, Queen Lydia, arrived. She wore a long tunic of copper-colored silk. Her auburn hair was held in place by a wreath of peach-colored roses. Midas's beautiful daughter, Ariel, skipped along at her mother's side. She wore a long white tunic. Her golden curls surrounded her face like a halo.

"Midas, what is all this?" Queen Lydia asked, scanning the crowded room in surprise.

"Just wait and see," Midas replied gleefully.

The king jumped up on a table and called for attention. "Welcome, guests, to the very first royal Phrygian music competition. Our judge will be none other than . . . Me!" Midas wagged his tail at the applause.

"Now let me introduce the contestants." He gestured with one paw. "In this corner, the immortal, the divine—and my good friend—Pan!"

The crowd cheered and applauded. Pan did a little jig and waved his flute.

"And in this corner—" Midas paused and looked around. "Who dares to challenge the forest god, anyway?"

A swirl of yellow smoke filled the room. The crowd drew back in awe. A handsome youth with golden curls stepped out of the smoke. He wore a sparkling gold tunic. In one hand he held a golden lyre—a small instrument like a harp.

The guests began to murmur. Midas licked his lips uncomfortably. *I've got a bad feeling about this,* he thought.

Pan stepped forward, his wooden flute under his arm. He bent low in a mock bow. "Well, well, well. Hello, Apollo."

The nobles gasped. The king swallowed hard. "Did you say *Apollo*? As in Apollo, the god of music?"

Queen Lydia's face lit up. "Apollo is going to play his lyre? How wonderful!" she exclaimed. "No, no! It's not wonderful at all!" Midas paced back and forth on the table. "How can I possibly keep my promise to Pan now?" he muttered.

"What promise, Daddy?" Ariel asked.

Midas paused to look fondly at his daughter. "Oh, it's nothing, really," he said weakly.

"All right, everybody. I'm here now, so let's get started," Apollo called in a booming voice. He raised his lyre above his head. The guests cheered. Midas gulped.

Apollo turned to Pan. "It looks as if this audience knows a winner when it sees one," he taunted. "Last chance, Pan. Are you sure you don't want to back out?"

Midas wagged his tail hopefully. "Hey, that's a great idea. What do you say, Pan? Maybe we should forget all about this contest and—"

"I wouldn't dream of backing out!" Pan interrupted. "We have promised this audience a contest." He gave Midas a sharp look. "And a promise is a promise."

The guests began to call for the show to start. Midas knew he was trapped. Finally, he waved his paw weakly. "Let the contest begin," he mumbled.

Pan stepped to the center of the room. The crowd fell silent as he began to pipe a light, happy shepherd's tune. His hooves tapped out the rhythm on the marble floor. The crowd clapped along, smiling. Midas looked around. Ariel and Lydia were dancing together. Midas thumped his tail to the beat. Hey, this song is great. In fact, it sounds like a winner to me, he thought with relief.

When Pan finished his tune, the king turned to the crowd. "Wasn't that terrific, folks? Let's have a round of applause for Pan!"

After the applause had died down, Apollo strode to the center of the room. He lifted his lyre and began to strum it. Soft, full notes filled the room. The nobles grew still. It was as if a trance had settled over everyone.

Midas listened and felt the music transport him like a dream. He saw himself chasing butterflies in a field. He felt the warm sun on his back and the soft grass beneath his paws.

> Apollo's music is fantastic! It sounds as if it's casting a spell over the audience—and over King Midas, too. Even though Pan's music was great, it didn't have such a strong effect, which means that Midas has a tough decision to make. It's not easy being in this guy's paws!

As the music went on, Midas saw Queen Lydia as she looked the day he had met her. He felt a shiver beneath his fur as their eyes met. How he loved her!

Then Midas saw Ariel as a tiny baby. How precious she was! His nostrils quivered as they filled with her sweet baby scent.

Finally, the notes died away. Apollo's song was over.

Midas let out his breath. It was easy to see how Apollo had gotten the music-god job. He looked around at the crowd. They stood in awed silence, unable even to applaud.

The spell was broken by Pan. The forest god stamped a hoof on the floor. He strode to the center of the room to stand beside Apollo. "All right, King Midas. It's time. You must declare a winner."

"A winner?" Midas echoed. His fur trembled. *Gods can be pretty creative with their revenge,* he thought nervously. *There could be some pretty scary stuff hidden in the fine print of that tablet I signed.*

Apollo stood beside Pan and waved his lyre. "Yes, King Midas," he said. "Who is the better musician?"

Midas cleared his throat. "Uh . . . yes . . . well . . . What do you say we all take a little break first? I'm sure everyone must be hungry. I know I am." Midas grabbed a hunk of meat from the table. He gobbled it down in one gulp. "Mmmm! Has anybody tried the pork?"

"Never mind the food!" Pan thundered. "Tell us who won, Midas."

"Yes, tell us," Apollo echoed. "Tell us who is the winner, Midas."

"The winner. Yes, of course, the winner." Midas licked his lips. "Hey, why do we need to choose a winner at all? After all, it's not whether you win or lose. It's how you play the game." He wagged his tail hopefully.

The two gods stepped closer to the king.

"You agreed to be the judge. It is your obligation to name a winner," Apollo said in a booming voice.

"That's right, Midas," Pan added with a sly smile. "You wouldn't want to forget your obligation, now would you, my friend?"

"Of-of c-course n-not," Midas stammered. "But first, let me say this. You both played really well. If I could, I'd name both of you winners. What I mean is—"

"Say the winner's name!" Apollo ordered.

Midas knew it was no use stalling any longer. "All right. The winner is . . . Pan."

A gasp of disbelief echoed around the room. Then the crowd began to murmur.

Apollo's face burned with sun-godly rage. He charged toward Midas. "How could you?" he yelled. "How could you choose his playing over mine?"

"It was a tough choice," Midas said quickly. "I mean your playing was fantastic, but . . ."

"You-you—" Apollo sputtered.

"Sorry, the judge's decisions are final. Party's over. Gotta go!" Midas hopped down from the table. He ran out of the room as fast as his four legs would carry him. He ducked into the first room he saw. It was his bedchamber.

But there was no escaping the furious sun god. Apollo appeared before him in a flash of yellow-orange smoke. Fiery sparks leaped from the god's eyes.

27

"Now simmer down," Midas said nervously. "We don't want anyone's whiskers to get singed."

Apollo let out a roar. Sparks flew from his mouth. "You think that amateur's piping was better than my playing? Then you must have something wrong with your ears!"

The sun god pointed his finger at Midas. Flames shot out of it. A hot orange cloud covered the king.

Midas choked on the smoke. He felt a strange tugging in his ears. Suddenly, his head felt heavy and out of balance.

"Hey, what happened?" the king asked. "Apollo, what did you do to me?"

But Apollo had vanished. Midas was alone.

The king turned around. He saw his reflection in a mirror. He gasped. Replacing Midas's handsome ears were the gigantic, hairy ears of a donkey! Midas threw his paws over his eyes in shame.

The following morning, King Midas awoke in his chamber. He raised a hind leg to scratch at his ear. Immediately, he remembered Apollo's curse. The enormous donkey ears were still firmly attached to his head.

There was a knock at the door. "Your Highness, it is Phidias, the royal hairdresser," a voice called. "I'm hear to prepare you for your tour of the kingdom."

I forgot all about the tour this afternoon, Midas thought. *I can't let anyone see me like this!*

"Your Highness, may I come in?" Phidias called.

Midas leaped down from the bed. "Just a

minute!" he yelled. He pawed through his wardrobe. Finally, he pulled out a huge hat that he had once worn to a festival. It was big enough to cover the donkey ears. Midas shoved it onto his head. "All right," he called. "You may come in."

Phidias stepped in. He wore a simple white tunic and held a leather satchel of tools. He stopped dead when he saw Midas's hat. Then he just stood there, staring.

"What's the matter, Phidias? Haven't you ever seen a hat before?" Midas snapped. He adjusted the hat as it began to slip sideways. He was having trouble balancing the enormous thing on his head.

"Of course, Your Highness," Phidias said. "It's just . . . do you plan to wear it on the tour?"

"As a matter of fact, yes, I do," Midas

29

replied. "I happen to like this hat a lot. A whole lot." *Like enough to wear it for the rest of my life*, he added silently.

Phidias looked doubtful. "If that is what Your Highness desires . . ." he said, his voice trailing off uncertainly.

Midas stretched out on a carpet. Phidias removed combs, brushes, and clippers from his bag. He paused and then with a puzzled look began to trim the few stray hairs that weren't covered by the hat.

Phidias paused and then took a deep breath. "Perhaps Your Highness would consider removing the hat just for a few moments," the hairdresser suggested gently.

Midas hesitated. Perhaps he could share his secret. After all, what harm could there be in telling just one person?

"I will take off my hat," Midas agreed. "But first you must promise never to tell anyone what you see here today. You must give me your word."

Phidias nodded. "I swear on my life I will not breathe a word to another human soul," he promised.

Midas removed his hat. Phidias clamped his hand over his mouth. He face turned red and he began to shake.

"Do you dare to laugh at your king?" Midas snapped.

"No, of course not," Phidias sputtered.

"Not at all." He took a deep breath to compose himself. "It's just . . . how?"

"Don't ask," Midas cut him off sharply. "And remember, you won't say a word about this to a single human soul."

Phidias nodded. But he still looked as if he were about to burst.

I hope he can be trusted, Midas thought.

The hairdresser quickly finished his work. Midas placed his hat back on his head. Then, he reminded Phidias once more of his promise before he dismissed him. Phidias nodded and left, his hand clamped over his mouth as if to keep the secret from spilling out.

Midas called for his servants. It was time for the royal tour to begin.

I don't know if I trust that Phidias. He's got a secret that seems pretty hard to keep! I have a feeling Midas might run into trouble on his journey. We'll catch up with him later. But what about Joe? Let's see how his efforts to be a successful businessman are going.

CHAPTER 4

"How's your new business going, Joe?" Ellen Talbot asked her son. The two were doing dishes in the kitchen after supper. Wishbone lay under the table, cleaning up a few stray crumbs.

"Great!" Joe exclaimed. "Miss Gilmore must have told everybody she knows about me. I've already got ten orders to fill by the end of the week." He reached for a dirty plate and dunked it in the sink full of soapy water.

"Hey, Joe, let me clean the plates," Wishbone offered. He covered his eyes with one paw. "I just can't watch perfectly good leftovers being washed down the drain."

"Ten orders?" Ellen said as she opened a cabinet filled with glasses and mugs. "That's great! How do you plan to make all those deliveries?"

"Well, I figure if I take my bike, it won't take too long," Joe said. "And if I get really big, then I can hire some people to work for me."

"Slow down!" Ellen laughed. "I think it's great

that you're already planning ahead, but let's start with the basics. How are you going to ride your bike and carry groceries at the same time?" Ellen asked. "I doubt you could carry more than a couple of bags on your handlebars."

Joe frowned. "I hadn't thought of that," he admitted. He rinsed off some silverware and dumped it onto the drainboard.

"I'll carry a bag for you, pal," Wishbone offered. "Of course, I might have to lighten the load a bit before I get started." He licked his lips.

Suddenly Joe's face brightened. "I know! You could drive me to my customers' houses," he suggested. "We could fit lots of bags in the backseat and the trunk of the car. I could pay you one dollar for each delivery."

"I don't think that's a good idea, Joe," Ellen said firmly. "This is your business, not mine. If you want to be a success, you need to do the work yourself."

"But, Mom—" Joe began to protest.

"I'm sorry, Joe, but that's the way it is. I have my own job at the library, and I don't ask for help with that. This is your business, not mine. You're in charge."

"I know," Joe said. He let the water drain out of the sink with a whoosh. "I'll think of a solution."

"I know you will," Ellen said. She gave Joe a reassuring pat on the shoulder. "Every business faces challenges at first. It's how you deal with those challenges that can help you succeed."

33

"Come on, Wishbone, let's go outside," Joe said. "We need to come up with a plan."

Wishbone followed Joe into the yard. "How about a nice game of fetch to help us think?" he suggested. But Joe wasn't paying attention. He went into the garage and stared at his bike.

"Uh, Joe, is there a reason you're just standing there?" Wishbone asked. He gently nudged Joe's hand with his nose. "It looks like the same old bike to me."

"Mom's right," Joe said to Wishbone. "I could not carry more than one or two bags on this bike."

Joe looked around the garage. "Hey, what's that?" he said suddenly. He hurried to a pile of objects stacked in the back of the garage.

Wishbone hurried over too. *Uh-oh, I hope Joe doesn't see those new tennis balls I chewed up last week,* Wishbone thought to himself. *I don't think he'd be too happy about that.*

But Joe had spotted something much more interesting than tennis balls. "Look, Wishbone! It's my old wagon," he said. He pulled a beat-up, red wagon out into the light. The wheels screeched in protest. "Mom used to pull me around in this when I was a little kid. A quick wash and some oil on the wheels, and this will be a great way to transport groceries around town."

Joe gave Wishbone a quick scratch between the ears as he pulled the wagon outside. "Mom was right," he said. "Dealing with challenges is just a way to make this business a success."

A few days later, Wishbone trotted around Joe's cozy bedroom, his nails clicking on the floor. He sniffed at the groceries stacked around the room. "Mmm, peanut butter, my favorite. Ooh, look, bologna! I say we open that first, Joe."

But Joe was busy consulting a list in his hand.

Wishbone hopped up onto the bed. A large glass jar sat on the plaid bedspread. Wishbone nosed it. "Hey, Joe, what's this? It doesn't smell like food." Inside the jar were a few bills and coins.

Beside the jar were several books from the Oakdale library. Samantha Kepler walked over and picked up one of the books. Sam, as she was called, was one of Joe's best friends. Her long, silky blond hair was pulled back into a ponytail. Like Wishbone, Sam was always in the mood for adventure. And she could always be counted on for a good scratch between the ears.

Sam read the title of the book out loud. *"Helping Your Small Business Grow Up."* She sat down on the bed and began to leaf through the book.

David Barnes selected another book from the pile. David was also one of Joe's best friends. He had dark, curly hair and brown eyes. A science whiz, David was always coming up with interesting inventions.

"Hey, look at this one," David said. *"Smile Your Way to the Bank: Ten Super Strategies for Service Industry Success."*

Joe continued organizing groceries into bags. "Aren't they great?" he said enthusiastically. He walked over to his desk on the far side of the room. He picked up another book. Many of its pages had been marked with bookmarks. "This is the best one. *Twenty Under Twenty: Teen Millionaires Share the Secrets of Their Success*. Listen to this." He leafed eagerly through the book until he found the passage he was looking for. "'Everyone has to start small, but nobody has to stay small.'"

Wishbone wagged his tail. "Hmmm . . . that could be the book for me."

Joe continued reading. "'The difference between the kid down the street who mows lawns for pocket change and the teenage millionaire is vision.'" He looked at his friends, his eyes shining.

David nodded. "So what's your vision, Joe?"

"Well, I've already grown five hundred percent in the last two weeks," Joe announced proudly.

"Really? You look the same size to me," Wishbone commented.

Sam's green eyes widened. "That's fantastic," she said.

David raised his eyebrows. "Hey, maybe we could help you," he suggested.

"Yeah," Sam added. "We can share the whole thing. That way it can be three times as big."

Joe nodded. "Actually, I wanted to offer you guys jobs," he replied. He grinned at them. "How does four dollars an hour sound?"

"Sure!" Sam said.

"Yeah!" David agreed.

"Great," Joe said. He glanced around his

cluttered room. "Okay, here are the lists. Once you get this food sorted into orders, there's some food in the freezer to add, too."

Sam and David hurried over to a stack of groceries and began sorting loaves of bread.

"Hey, what about a job for the cute little dog?" Wishbone asked. "Like maybe . . . taste tester?"

Joe watched his friends with a smile. He picked up another book and began to read.

"You could pay me in food," Wishbone went on.

Sam cleared her throat. "Hey, Joe, aren't you going to help us?" she asked.

"Actually, I'm trying to learn how to delegate," Joe said. He shrugged. "According to all the books, that's what authority is all about."

"Delegate, huh? I prefer the paws-on approach when it comes to working with food." Wishbone's stomach growled. He looked up at Joe. "Hey, boss, when do we get our lunch break?"

But Joe was too interested in his book to notice.

It looks as if Joe's pretty involved in that book of his. He's determined to make his business a big success. Being a big success was pretty important to King Midas, too. In fact, you might say it was too important. . . .

CHAPTER
5

Midas perched on a silk cushion on the royal traveling throne. Phidias had groomed his fur to perfection. He wore one of his best robes. It was finely woven of pale yellow fabric trimmed in gold. Midas always liked

Lots of kings toured their kingdoms. These tours were called royal progresses. Although Midas is just taking a short tour, some tours lasted for weeks, or even months! Touring the kingdom was important because it gave the king a firsthand look at how things were going. And the king's subjects were pretty excited to talk to royalty. Meeting the king personally helped those subjects stay loyal. That was good for the kingdom, too.

to look his best on his tours through the kingdom.

Four young servants carried the throne. They were simply dressed for the hot day. White cloths were tied around their waists, and leather sandals protected their feet. The throne bumped as the servants carried it along the rocky road. Midas was careful to balance his large hat on his head as the throne moved along.

Midas breathed in the fresh smells of the Phrygian countryside. Touring the kingdom was one of his favorite things to do.

His fur tingled with excitement as he spotted a small farming and fishing village up ahead. *I recognize this place*, he realized. *This is where Phidias, the royal hairdresser, lives.*

The road was already crowded with people waiting to greet their king. As Midas was carried into the village, a great cheer went up from the crowd. Midas nodded and waved a paw regally at them. "Hello, helllooo, everyone! Your king greets you!" he thought as he hopped off his throne.

He stopped in front of two farmers. "How are you?" he asked them.

"Sire," the first farmer said, "we are praying to the goddess Demeter for a big crop of corn."

"Well, let's hope Demeter is all ears," Midas said.

The farmers laughed loudly.

Midas spotted Phidias among the well-wishers. The hairdresser no longer had his hand clamped over his mouth. In fact, Phidias looked much more relaxed than the last time Midas had seen him. Midas waved him over.

"You haven't told anyone our little secret, have you?" Midas whispered.

"I swore to you that I would not tell another human soul, and I've kept my promise," he said gravely.

"Good, good," Midas replied. He turned back to the crowd and saw a group of fishermen dressed in simple, rough tunics. They carried handwoven nets full of fish. The group seemed to be laughing behind their hands.

Wow, everyone's in a great mood today, Midas thought. His tail wagged. *The farmers liked my corn joke. Let's see if I can think of a good fishing joke.*

"Why did the fish cross the river?" Midas asked.

The fishermen laughed harder than ever. Their faces turned bright red.

"I haven't even gotten to the punch line yet," Midas said in surprise. "Okay, are you ready? Why did the fish cross the river? Because the road was too crowded with chickens." The fishermen roared with laughter. A few wiped tears from their eyes.

A servant leaned close to Midas. "Your Highness," he whispered, "we must move on. Otherwise we will not have time to complete the tour by sundown."

"All right," Midas said reluctantly. He saw several of the fishermen still laughing. *We certainly seem to have some silly fishermen here,* Midas thought. *Did someone put a laughing potion in the river?*

Midas made his way back through the crowd, nodding to the smiling people. Finally, Midas reached his throne and settled onto the soft cushions. "On to the next village," he commanded.

The servants carried the throne down the road. Midas breathed in the smells of trees and grass. He settled back, his nose on his paws.

Suddenly Midas's sharp hearing picked up a strange sound. It sounded like a low moaning. What is that? he wondered. It's coming from somewhere just ahead.

Midas sat up straight and peered forward. After a moment, he spotted someone lying in a ditch at the side of the road. It looked like an old man with

41

a white beard. The man's blue robe was ripped and splattered with mud.

"Halt!" Midas called.

The servants stopped at once.

"Who is that?" Midas lifted a paw toward the crumpled, motionless man.

One of the servants glanced at the side of the road. "Oh, that's just some worthless old man who's drunk himself into a ditch," he said with a shrug.

Midas sniffed the air. Mingling with the scent of mud was something else. Something familiar.

"Let me down," the king commanded.

The servants set down the throne. Midas hopped off and trotted over to the edge of the road.

The king nosed the man in the ditch. Then he jumped back in surprise. "I know this man! This is Silenus. He is a wise man, a teacher, and a friend of the gods." Midas peered closely at the old man. "He isn't drunk. He's been beaten."

Silenus's eyelids fluttered. He managed to lift his head. "And robbed," he said weakly. "I have nothing now. And I have no way to get home."

King Midas placed a paw gently on the old man's shoulder. "Don't worry, my friend. I will help you."

Midas called to his servants. "We cannot leave this man lying here. Place him on my seat!"

The servants quickly lifted the old man onto the throne.

"Be careful," Midas told them. "Silenus is an important man. You know, he was the first teacher of Bacchus, the god of food, drink, and merriment." *Just a few of my favorite things*, he thought.

"Where shall we take him?" one of the servants asked.

"Back to the palace," Midas instructed them. "The rest of the royal tour will have to wait for another day."

The servants turned around and headed back up the road. Midas trotted alongside.

Poor Silenus, Midas thought. *It's a good thing I came along when I did. We'll get him cleaned up and back in shape in no time.*

When they arrived back at the palace, the servants carried Silenus inside. "Bring him to the largest guest chamber, down the hall from my own," Midas commanded.

Queen Lydia passed them in the hallway. A startled expression crossed her face when she saw the injured man.

"Lydia!" King Midas called eagerly. "Look who I have brought! It is Silenus. You know, Bacchus's old teacher."

"You're hurt! You poor man!" Lydia exclaimed, bending over Silenus.

"Don't worry, dear. I will see that he gets cleaned up," Midas replied. "And I'll send for the royal physician at once."

At last they arrived in the guest chamber. The servants placed Silenus gently on the bed.

"Bring him some water to wash with," Midas ordered. "Bring some fresh robes, too."

The servants hurried out of the room to do as Midas asked. Midas watched with concern as the royal physician treated Silenus and the servants helped the old man into clean clothes. "Will he be all right?" Midas asked the doctor.

"Yes, he'll be fine after a few days of rest," the physician assured him. "He has some nasty cuts on his head and bruises on his arms and legs. He has a cracked rib, too," the physician added as he wound a bandage tightly around Silenus's chest.

Silenus turned to Midas. "Thank you so much for your help," he said weakly. "I don't know what would have happened if you hadn't come along when you did. Good King Midas, you have saved my life. I am indebted to you forever."

"Oh, don't mention it," Midas said with a wave of his paw. "On the other hand, go ahead and mention it to anyone you want." *After all,* he thought, *it wouldn't hurt to have Bacchus know about what I did for his old teacher.*

"In fact," Midas continued, "is there anyone you'd like to contact, Silenus? How about one of your old students?" Midas paused and wagged his tail eagerly. "Hey, I know! How about Bacchus?"

"Bacchus?" Silenus said in surprise. "I haven't seen him in ages."

"Really?" Midas's tail drooped. *Oh well, nice try,* he thought. "We'll leave you to rest now. I'll stop in to see you later."

A few days later, Silenus was feeling much better.

He and Midas were sharing a hearty lunch when Midas had a great idea. "Why don't we have a party to celebrate your recovery?" he suggested. "Not to mention my own wisdom in recognizing who you were," Midas added, puffing out his chest.

"Oh, no, I don't know if I am feeling up to a party," Silenus said. "Thanks for asking, but I really don't think—"

"Oh, come on, Silenus, it will be fun!" Midas urged. "It will lift your spirits. I'll invite everyone of importance in the kingdom, and you can invite all your friends, too. We should ask your old students to attend." *One student in particular*, Midas added to himself.

"I don't want to put you through any trouble . . ." Silenus began.

"It's no trouble at all!" Midas said.

"It *would* be nice to see some of my old friends again," Silenus said with a smile.

"Great, it's decided then. We'll have a big party." The more Midas thought about it, the more he liked the idea. After this big celebration, everyone in the kingdom would be talking about how he had rescued Silenus. They might even forget about that silly music contest.

Midas stood up and began to run around in excited circles. "It will be the greatest party I've ever had! We'll have the best food, the meatiest bones . . ."

And who knows? Midas added silently. Bacchus himself might even decide to show up. After all, he was the original party animal!

Midas sure has high hopes for his big party. And Joe has high hopes for his new business. Let's take a look and see how Joe's doing.

CHAPTER
6

Wishbone stared at the long line of grocery bags on the floor in the Talbots' sunny kitchen. The brown paper bags seemed to go on forever. And the counters and kitchen table were covered with food. Wishbone had never seen so much food in one place in his whole life. He couldn't take his eyes off the row of bags. His nose was filled with dozens of delicious smells.

"I think I'm in heaven," Wishbone said, staring at the huge array of food.

Joe moved down the line of bags, loading more food into each one. As he packed the various items, he checked them off on the lists on the bags. "Wishbone, this is our biggest day yet," he said happily. "Can you believe all these orders?"

Wishbone shook his head. "You mean, this isn't all for us?" he asked. His tail drooped in disappointment.

Nearby, Sam sat on the floor. In front of her was a large bunch of yellow-and-white daisies. Wishbone watched as Sam carefully separated the

47

flowers into smaller bunches. Then she wrapped each bunch in a sheet of green tissue paper.

Sam stood up, a satisfied smile on her face. She made her way down the line of grocery bags, placing a small bouquet in each bag.

When she was finished, Sam stepped back to admire her work. "Don't these look pretty?" she asked.

"They're beautiful, Sam." Wishbone sniffed at a daisy. "Let me know if you run out of flowers. I can always run next door to Wanda's and dig some up."

Sam turned to Joe. "Do you think the customers will like these?" she asked.

Joe paused, a bag of grapes in his hand. He studied the flowers. A big smile crossed his face.

"Those are terrific, Sam!" he exclaimed.

Sam grinned.

"It's a brilliant strategy," Joe went on. His eyes shone with excitement. "I was just reading about this in one of my books. It's very important to create the impression of a personal relationship with the customer. Including flowers is a brilliant marketing strategy."

"Marketing strategy?" Sam looked surprised. "I was just trying to be nice."

Joe didn't answer. He was too busy consulting a grocery list on one of the bags.

A little while later, the bags were all packed. Joe's mother, Ellen, poked her head in. "My goodness, look at all this," she said. "You must have spent hours shopping for all these orders, Joe," she said.

Joe smiled. "But isn't it great?"

"Yes, but don't forget your homework. Didn't you say you had a big social studies paper coming up?"

Joe frowned. "Uh, right, the social studies paper. Don't worry, Mom. It's not due for a while. And once we get these orders out, I'll have plenty of time for social studies."

"Okay." Ellen said. "I'm going back to work. See you later."

Sam and Joe brought the first of their deliveries outside to the driveway. Wishbone trotted after them.

Wishbone sniffed the warm air. "Hey, where's David? Our pack isn't complete without him."

Sam looked around. "Where's David? Wasn't he supposed to meet us here?"

Wishbone sighed. "Helllooo! Didn't I just ask that? Doesn't anybody listen to the dog?"

Joe glanced at his watch. "He'd better get here soon. We have a ton of deliveries to make today."

"I'll be glad to take care of any leftover inventory," Wishbone said, licking his lips.

A moment later, Wishbone's ears picked up the sound of a bicycle approaching. David coasted to a stop in the driveway, brakes squeaking.

Wishbone stared at David's bike in surprise. Attached to the back was a large wooden wagon with slatted sides. The wagon rested on two bicycle wheels.

"Hmmm . . . this definitely calls for an investigation. Don't go away," Wishbone told the closest bag of groceries. "I'll be back for you later."

The little dog trotted down the driveway. Joe and Sam were right behind him.

David grinned and waved. "What do you think?" he asked.

"Wow!" Sam exclaimed.

"Cool!" Joe added.

"Uh, sure," Wishbone said. "I just have one question. What is it?"

David smiled, still straddling the bicycle. He pointed back to the sign on the side of the wagon. It read JOE'S GROCERY DELIVERY BRINGS HOME THE BACON. "Our grocery delivery cart," he said proudly.

"Oh, right," Wishbone said. "I knew that."

"My dad and I built it," David said. "This cart can hold nine bags of groceries."

"Wow! That's a lot more than I can load into my old wagon," Joe said.

"This cart looks a lot nicer than that beat-up old thing too," David said.

Sam grinned. "It looks as if there's even room for Wishbone back there."

Wishbone trotted around the cart. "Okay, save me a seat next to the salami."

Joe nodded, eyes shining. "This is great!"

"It wouldn't take long to build two more," David suggested. "Then we could deliver more groceries faster."

Joe's eyes grew even brighter. A huge grin crossed his face. "Yes! And that means more money!"

A few days later the other two grocery carts were finished. Joe and Sam stood in David's driveway with their bikes. Wishbone sat nearby, watching.

David squatted by Sam's bike. He held a screwdriver in his hand. "Okay, Sam, I'll have the cart attached to your bike in no time," he promised. "Then I'll do yours, Joe."

Wishbone jumped up into Joe's waiting wagon. "Ready when you are!" he called. "Let's get those groceries in here."

Joe checked his watch. "We'd better hurry. We still have to pick up the groceries at the store and organize everything before we start our deliveries."

"Hey, Joe, isn't your basketball team having dinner at Pepper Pete's tonight?" Sam asked.

"Yeah," Joe sighed. "I really wanted to go. But the business has to come first!"

"I guess so," Sam said.

A few minutes later, Joe's cart was ready. Joe, David, and Sam all climbed on their bikes.

"Let's go!" Joe said with a grin.

Wishbone felt the wind in his fur as Joe began pedaling. The three friends took off down the driveway and turned onto the road. Together they raced toward the supermarket, their carts rattling along behind them.

Wishbone dug his claws into the floor of the wooden wagon. His whole body bounced as the cart bumped along. His ears flapped in the breeze.

"Whee!" he yelled happily. "What a way to travel. Yahoo!"

A few evenings later, Joe sat at the wooden desk in his room. His social studies book lay open on the desk. Joe rubbed his eyes tiredly.

Wishbone lay on the bed. "Whew, another long day of deliveries," he said. "I'm dog-tired."

Just then, Sam and David appeared in the doorway. "Hey, Joe, what's up?" Sam asked.

"Yeah, what's up?" David echoed. "You don't look very happy."

"Oh, it's nothing. I'm just trying to squeeze in some work on that social studies paper." Joe frowned. "And I just got off the phone with one of the guys from the team. They're all mad because I missed the dinner the other night."

"That's too bad," Sam said sympathetically.

"Maybe you should—"

"Hey, look at this," Joe interrupted. His face brightened as he picked up a large glass jar stuffed with money. A label on the jar read PROFITS.

"There are two hundred and sixty dollars in here. Can you believe it? And we're getting more customers every day."

"All right!" David said. Sam leaned over to give Joe a high-five. Then she sat down beside Wishbone on the bed.

"Hey, Sam, how about a scratch?" Wishbone asked hopefully. Obligingly, Sam began rubbing his ears. "Ooh, that feels good. A little to the left . . ."

"Listen, you guys have been really great," Joe told his friends. "I want to give you something. I really want to . . . uh . . . recognize your achievements, and . . ."

Joe paused, as if he had forgotten what he wanted to say. He picked up one of his business books and quickly flipped through the pages. "Oh yes . . . and show you that you're important members of the Joe's Grocery Delivery family," he finished.

Joe closed the book. He reached for two long white envelopes on his desk.

David and Sam glanced at each other curiously. David raised his eyebrows. Sam just shrugged.

Wishbone sat up. "Hey, what about my bonus? A package of hot dogs would be fine. I'm sure I saw one around here earlier. We don't have to give all the food to the customers, do we?"

Joe handed each of his friends an envelope. "Go

on, open them," he said eagerly.

Sam and David quickly tore at their envelopes. Sam pulled out a sheet of paper. She unfolded it and began to read. The excitement on her face drained away, replaced by a look of confusion.

David stared at the identical paper in his hands. Wishbone padded to the edge of the bed for a better look. David looked at the form letter with his name written in.

"A Certificate of Contribution?" David said.

Joe nodded enthusiastically.

Sam cleared her throat. "'Certificate of Contribution awarded in appreciation to Samantha Kepler . . .'" she read.

"' . . . for hard work, diligence, and devotion to Joe's Grocery Delivery,'" David finished.

Silence filled the room.

"Uh, thanks, Joe," Sam said at last.

"Yeah, thanks a lot," David said. He didn't sound too excited.

"This is really . . . thoughtful," Sam added.

Wishbone gazed back and forth between Sam's and David's faces. "Don't worry, Joe. Underneath those glum faces, I'm sure they're just thrilled."

Speaking of being thrilled, that's exactly how Midas felt about his party plans. And he was thrilled with himself for having rescued Silenus. Little did he know the trouble his bright idea was about to cause.

CHAPTER 7

"So I said, 'That's no ordinary old man. That's Silenus!'" Midas told the group of nobles around him. "I knew it right away, you see."

Midas sat in his favorite chair with the softest cushions in the palace's great hall. He wore his best white silk robe, sewn through with golden threads. His large hat was balanced on his head.

A woman in a pale blue robe waved a jeweled and feathered fan in front of her face and let out a sigh of admiration. "Our King Midas will surely go down in history as a great ruler."

The king's tail wagged happily. "Ah, but you've heard enough of my stories," he said. "Go on. Enjoy the party. Eat, drink, and be merry!" *Just as Bacchus would do if he were here,* Midas thought.

The crowd broke up. People headed for the banquet tables, which were groaning under their heavy platters of food. King Midas glanced around the room, his brown eyes shining with pleasure. All the most important people in Phrygia were there.

> **Nobody knew how to throw a party like the ancient Greeks. They had so much food and drink at their parties, I bet I couldn't even eat it all! The feasting could go on all night and into the next day. Now *that's* what I call a party!**

The most delicious foods were laid out on the tables. The musicians were playing their best tunes. *Is this a party or what?* thought Midas.

He spotted a servant leading a group of merchants toward the kitchen. Two of the merchants held baskets heaped high with fish. Midas trotted over to them. "I hope this fish is fresh," he said.

"It certainly is, Your Highness," one of them replied, starting to snicker. "We got it straight from the fishermen at the Pyrite River." He let out a large guffaw.

The other merchant managed to pull himself together. "Don't mind him, Your Highness," he said. "He's still laughing over a little joke we heard at the river."

At these words, the first merchant began to laugh even harder.

The king's brown eyes opened wide. "Oh, I get it," he said after a moment, remembering the silly fishermen he'd met in the village. *They were in stitches over my jokes. I suppose they've been passing*

them along to everyone they meet. "You know, I'm probably the one responsible for that little joke you heard," Midas told the merchants proudly.

"I should say you are, Sire!" the first merchant burst out. He laughed so hard that tears rolled down his cheeks.

The other man tugged on his robe. "We'd better be going, Your Highness. We've got to get these fish to the kitchen right away."

Midas watched as the two men hurried off. He wondered if all the fish merchants in his kingdom were as silly as those two.

His thoughts were interrupted by the sight of his daughter, Ariel, walking toward him. The princess wore a special tunic of cream-colored silk for the occasion.

> **Ariel sounds like someone who enjoys her food. Now there's a girl after my own heart!**

"Daddy, this is so much fun!" the little girl said. Her face shone with happiness. "And the sugared figs are delicious. I already had five of them!"

Midas reached out a paw and gently touched her shoulder. "Now, don't eat too many, my darling."

In the far corner of the room, Midas spotted more guests arriving. He gave his daughter a kiss and trotted over to great the newcomers.

Hours later, the celebration was still going

strong. Everyone was having a great time, but Midas couldn't help feeling a bit disappointed.

I hoped that Bacchus might drop by, he thought. *He's supposed to be a regular bloodhound when it comes to sniffing out parties. And I even have Silenus here.*

Midas spotted the old man heading toward the guest chambers. "Wait, Silenus!" Midas cried, trotting toward him. "Where are you going?"

"Off to bed. I'm feeling a bit tired," Silenus answered. He rubbed his eyes and yawned. "I plan to be on my way tomorrow, so I need my rest. But I thank you for your generous hospitality."

"But you can't leave yet! You're the guest of honor," Midas said. *And if you leave, Bacchus will probably never come,* he added silently. "I know!" He clapped his paws. "Let's have a toast!"

> When Midas talks about a toast, he doesn't mean a piece of bread. Toasts are a way to praise a special guest at a party. Everyone holds his or her drink up while the host says something nice about the guest of honor. Then all the guests swallow their drink to show they agree with the praise. Quite a fun custom, I think!

A servant brought Silenus and Midas goblets. Midas turned to face his guests. "A toast! To our guest of honor, Silenus," he said loudly. "And to his greatest student, Bacchus!"

"Here! Here!" the guests cried, raising their glasses.

Midas looked around, his tail wagging eagerly. There was still no sign of Bacchus.

Suddenly Midas felt a soft touch on the back of his neck. He turned and saw Queen Lydia standing behind him.

"I'm taking Ariel to bed," she told him. "And I'm going to bed myself. I'm very tired."

"What? So early? But the party has just begun!" Midas protested.

"Midas, we've been here for hours and hours. This is already the longest party Phrygia has ever seen," Lydia pointed out. "It's very late. Look, our guests are all leaving."

Midas surveyed the room. The crowds of people were slowly making their way toward the doors. "I suppose you're right," he admitted. *Oh well, I guess it doesn't matter if Bacchus didn't show*, he added to himself. After all, this was a party the nobles of Phrygia would be talking about for months to come!

The following afternoon, Midas sat in the palace's main chamber, working on a tasty new lamb bone. Except for his ear problem, he was quite a contented king.

At this very moment, he thought, *all of Phrygia is talking about my great party and my rescue of Silenus. Not to mention that the fishermen in town think I'm a regular laugh riot. Besides that, I have a juicy lamb*

bone, a soft, comfortable throne to chew it on, and a happy, healthy family who loves me. He sighed contentedly. All was well.

Suddenly a thick cloud of purple smoke billowed into the room. Midas lifted his head from his bone and sniffed. The cloud smelled delicious. Midas's mouth watered at the scent.

A few moments later, the cloud cleared away. Standing before Midas was an enormous, stout man draped in rich purple robes. The man had short, dark curls surrounded by a wreath of green vines and leaves. In his hand, he held a giant turkey drumstick, dripping with juice.

Mmmm, Midas thought, eyeing the meaty drumstick. *Want to trade bones?* Then his eyes

grew wide as he recognized his visitor. "Bacchus? Is it really you?"

The god nodded, his mouth still stuffed with turkey. He swallowed noisily. "Sorry I missed the party," he said. "I was already double-booked."

"I understand," Midas said. "You're a busy god."

Bacchus nodded. "You're not kidding. I had a wedding in Apollonia and a fiftieth anniversary party in Thebes. But I did want to make an appearance here to thank you personally, Midas. That was a great thing you did for Silenus. He was my favorite teacher back in my school days. He told the most interesting stories! I'm glad that you rescued him."

Midas's tail wagged happily. "My pleasure, O godly one."

Bacchus wiped his mouth with the back of his hand. He let out a belch, and a tiny cloud of purple smoke escaped from his mouth. He looked around and snapped his fingers twice.

Several servants appeared out of thin air behind the god. Each one carried a heaping dish of food.

Wow! What a neat trick! Midas thought. "Hey, could you teach me how to do that?" he asked.

Bacchus didn't answer. Instead, he snapped his fingers. A servant holding a bulging cluster of purple grapes stepped forward. The servant plucked one grape and dropped it into Bacchus's mouth.

Bacchus chewed with great relish. He wiped the juice from his mouth. Then he snapped his fingers again. Another servant stepped forward with a purple linen napkin. The god spit the pit from his grape into the napkin, and the servant stepped back.

Bacchus swallowed. "So where is Silenus? I hope I didn't miss him."

"He left this morning," Midas said.

"Oh well, no matter." Bacchus waved his hand in the air. "It's really you I've come to see."

"Me?" Midas's tail wagged happily. "Great!"

Bacchus bit off another hunk of his drumstick. "I wif to fank you for what you did for Filenus," he said through a mouthful of food.

"What? Oh, you're welcome," Midas said. "It was my pleasure, really. You know me. I'm always ready to do anything I can to make the gods happy."

"I'd like to give you something in return," Bacchus continued.

"That's great." Midas licked his lips. "How about starting with a piece of that turkey?"

Bacchus grinned. "Midas, you have pleased me greatly. To thank you, and to express my divine appreciation, I will grant you . . ."

He paused dramatically and glanced back at his servants. One of them pulled a small drum from his robes and began a drumroll.

" . . . one wish!" Bacchus finished.

"A wish?" Midas cocked his ears. "You mean anything?"

Bacchus nodded. "Anything."

"Oh, wow! Oh, wow!" Midas was so excited, he jumped up and did a flip in the air. "This is so great! Let me think. I've already got a wonderful wife, a darling daughter, and a happy kingdom. What should I wish for?"

Ideas dog-paddled around and around Midas's head. *Fame? Fortune? A lifetime supply of big, juicy steaks?*

Midas scratched his ears with his hind leg and felt the enormous hat balanced on his head. This would be a good chance to get rid of the donkey ears. But he didn't want to waste his wish on something like that. After all, this is the opportunity of a lifetime!

Suddenly Midas thought of something that would make him richer than anyone on earth. And it was something that would make him famous throughout the empire. It was a power worthy of one of the gods themselves.

"I've got it!" Midas announced. "I wish—"

"Take your time," Bacchus interrupted. He raised a finger in warning. "Think about it carefully."

"I wish for the golden touch!" Midas said, ignoring Bacchus's warning.

Bacchus's smile faded. "You do?" he asked.

"That's right," Midas said. He was proud of his bright idea. "I wish that everything I touch would turn into gold."

Bacchus sighed. He seemed very disappointed. "All right. If you say so," he said.

As Midas watched, the god waved his hand in the air. Once again, Midas was enveloped in a cloud of purple smoke.

Have you ever heard the saying, "Be careful what you wish for, because you just might get it"? Well, Midas has made quite a wish, and some pretty incredible things are going to happen to him because of it. But what about Joe? He wished for his business to be successful. Is his wish coming true as well? Let's find out.

CHAPTER
8

I t was a warm spring evening. Joe coasted his bike to a stop in front of the bulletin board at the Community Center. Wishbone trotted along behind him. Joe was on his way to the library to work on his big social studies project with Sam.

"Wow! Look at that!" Joe exclaimed.

In the center of the Community Center bulletin board was a huge ad for Joe's Grocery Delivery. It featured a picture of Joe hugging Wanda Gilmore. Beneath the picture were the words, "I'm a satisfied customer of Joe's Grocery Delivery. He's hardworking, reliable, and honest. Call Joe today to handle all your shopping needs!"

Below the picture had been a row of twenty tags printed with Joe's name and the Talbots' phone number. Every one of the tags was gone.

"That's twenty new potential customers for my business," Joe said happily. "We're growing at an amazing rate. Maybe I will be a millionaire while I'm still in my teens!"

Wishbone eyed a little boy and his mother

sitting on a nearby bench. The boy was licking a huge vanilla ice-cream cone. The mother had a tiny baby bundled up on her lap.

"Hey, Joe, if you're going to be a millionaire, you should invest your money wisely. I think ice cream is the way to go," Wishbone said.

"Excuse me. Are you Joe Talbot?" asked the boy's mother.

Joe straightened up and walked toward her. "Yes. I'm Joe Talbot of Joe's Grocery Delivery," he said. He extended one hand for her to shake. "What can I do for you?"

Wishbone settled down at the little boy's feet. The boy leaned down and patted him happily on the head, leaving a sticky smear of vanilla ice cream on Wishbone's nose.

"Thanks, pal," Wishbone said, swiping his nose clean with his long, pink tongue. "Feel free to pet me any time."

You're the answer to my prayers," the woman said. "I've heard great things about your delivery service."

"Would you like to become a customer?" Joe asked.

"Yes, I would. Things have been so hectic since my new baby was born. I need to go shopping, but I'm just too tired. And it's nice to just sit and enjoy the evening with my children. I have my shopping list and the money right here. Would you go to the store for me right now? I live just around the corner."

"Another trip to the grocery store?" Wishbone

asked. His tail thumped happily against the sidewalk. "Sounds good to me!"

"Well, it's kind of late," Joe said. "I could stop by tomorrow afternoon—"

"No, I really need the groceries tonight. We're out of everything!" the woman said with an apologetic smile. "Listen, I'll throw in an extra ten dollars for you. And I'm sure I'll become a regular customer."

"Well . . . okay," Joe said. He smiled. "At Joe's Grocery Delivery, we never let a customer down!"

"Great!" The woman dug around in her purse and pulled out a list and a wad of money. She jotted down her address on the back of the shopping list. "See you soon."

Joe hopped back on his bike. "Come on, Wishbone. We've got work to do!" he called.

Two hours later, Joe pedaled home slowly. Wishbone snoozed in the back of the Joe's Grocery Delivery cart. It was completely dark now, and the air was cool.

"That lady sure was happy to get her groceries," Joe said as he turned into his driveway. "And you know what? I'll bet she'll tell her friends about Joe's Grocery Delivery, and we'll get even more business—and more money! Things are going so great!"

Wishbone sat up and sniffed. He smelled a familiar scent. Then he saw some familiar faces. "Uh, Joe? If things are going so well, why are Sam and your mother sitting on your

67

front porch, looking so unhappy?"

"Joe? Where have you been?" Ellen called.

"Yeah, Joe, where have you been?" Sam echoed. She sounded annoyed.

"Sam! What are you doing here?" Joe asked. "I thought you were at the library . . . oh, no!"

"I was at the library," Sam said tersely. "I was working on our social studies paper. You know, the one you're supposed to be working on, too? The one you were supposed to meet me to work on tonight?"

"I forgot," Joe admitted. Wishbone jumped out of the cart and went to sit beside Ellen on the porch as Joe walked slowly up the steps.

"I was so worried when Sam said you hadn't shown up at the library. Where were you?" Ellen asked as she scratched behind Wishbone's ears.

"I had to get groceries for a new customer," Joe said. He quickly explained the events of the evening. "I just couldn't let her down, Mom."

"I'm glad you're so responsible, Joe. But you can't let yourself down, either," Ellen said.

"Or your friends," Sam said.

"I know. I'm really sorry," Joe said. "Can we get together after dinner tomorrow night, Sam? I promise I'll show up this time."

"Yeah, come on, Sam," Wishbone agreed. He looked up at her and added, "Give Joe one more chance."

"All right," Sam said. She smiled and patted Wishbone on the head. "I'll see you tomorrow. Bye, Mrs. Talbot," she said as she got up and headed for home.

Joe started into the house. "Just a minute," Ellen said, holding out a hand to stop him.

"What is it, Mom?"

"Are you sure you can handle your business *and* school *and* your friends?" Ellen asked with concern.

"Of course I can," Joe said. "Mom, this business is really important to me. I want it to be a success, and I'm willing to work hard to do it."

"I know that, and I'm proud of you," Ellen said. "But school and friends are important too. Don't forget, there are lots of ways to be successful without being a millionaire. And your schoolwork has to come first."

"I know. I can do it, Mom. I'm going to go inside and study right now," Joe promised.

Wishbone barked in agreement. "How about a snack first?" he suggested. "Studying is hard work, you know!"

Joe certainly has the golden touch when it comes to his business. But sometimes you can have way too much of a good thing . . . as Midas is about to find out!

CHAPTER
9

When the smoke cleared, Bacchus was gone. Midas looked around. His gaze stopped when he saw the floor. The gray stone had turned into shining gold beneath his paws!

The hat on his head suddenly seemed very heavy. Midas raised a paw to feel it. It, too, had turned to solid gold!

"Wow, this is incredible!" Midas lowered his nose to the floor. "Hey, I can see myself! This looks great. We should have put a gold floor in here years ago."

Midas trotted across the golden floor to the far end of the room. Two low, carved wooden tables stood against a wall. He placed a paw on one, then the other. Both turned instantly to gold.

"Amazing! I can turn anything to gold. Anything at all!" Midas's tail wagged with excitement. "I know. How about some gold chairs to go with the gold tables?"

He ran across the room, skidding on the gold

floor. A row of carved wooden chairs stood against a wall. One by one he nosed the chairs, turning them into carved gold as well.

"Whee! This is so much fun!" Midas did a flip in the air. "Just think. We can have an all-gold palace!"

Midas looked around. "Okay, we need a gold vase here . . . and some gold rugs . . . and how about some gold tapestries, too?" Midas ran happily through the palace, touching everything in sight. "Gold walls, gold draperies, gold candles . . . oops! I guess gold candles won't burn very well, will they? Oh well, they look good."

Midas surveyed the room, panting from all his running around. Everything gleamed with gold.

Suddenly the king thought of his wife. *I must show all this to Lydia! She's not going to believe my wonderful new power.*

Midas knew Queen Lydia liked to spend the afternoons in one of the royal rose gardens. He trotted to the door. The king's paws kept sliding out from under him. *This gold floor is pretty slippery*, he realized.

Outside, Midas squinted in the sunlight. The ground felt hard and strange beneath his paws. He looked down and laughed. "Even the dirt I'm standing on has been turned to tiny gold nuggets. This is fantastic!"

As Midas walked across the ground, tiny bits of gold got stuck under his nails. He shook his paws out impatiently. *It's an inconvenience*, he thought, *but a small price to pay for my amazing new power.* Midas loved the way the gold spread out along the ground as he trotted along. His tail wagged happily.

Midas stopped to sniff a nearby tree. Before his eyes, the tree—bark, branches, leaves, and all— turned entirely to gold at the touch of his wet nose.

The king gazed up at the tree, which now shimmered in the sunlight. "Gold trees! This is great! I'll have the only gold forest in Phrygia—no, in the whole empire! In the whole world! Everyone will know the name of Midas now."

Midas ran from garden to garden, searching for Lydia. As he ran along, everything turned to gold at the touch of his paws.

Finally he found the queen. Lydia was sitting on a marble bench. She waved a feathered fan back and forth gently to cool herself.

"Lydia, my dear!" Midas called. As he trotted toward her, the stone path beneath his feet turned to gold. The queen stared at the golden stones in astonishment.

"Isn't it fantastic?" exclaimed the king.

Queen Lydia looked shocked. "But how?"

"It's my special new power," Midas explained happily. "It was granted to me by Bacchus himself. It's sort of a divine thank-you card for saving Silenus."

Lydia still looked doubtful. "What you did for Silenus was very kind. But why did Bacchus choose to thank you in this way?"

"Actually, I chose it myself," Midas replied. "Bacchus granted me one wish. So I picked the golden touch. Pretty clever, eh? Watch this!" Midas nosed a small wooden bench. It turned instantly to gold.

"That's amazing," the queen said. "I can hardly believe my eyes. No mortal man has ever done anything like it."

"I know," Midas replied happily. "Now look at this." He put his paw on a small fence. It, too, turned instantly to gold. "Oh, Lydia, do you know what this means? We're the luckiest people on earth!"

"Midas, we were already lucky," Lydia pointed out. "We have our family, our health, a happy kingdom—"

Midas barely heard her words. "Watch this!" He put his paw on a stone, which turned to gold. "And look at this!" He nosed a patch of grass. The golden blades shimmered in the sunlight. "And this!" He ran toward a rose bush and brushed it with his head.

"No!" the queen objected. "Not my beautiful roses! Please!"

But it was too late. The golden bush shimmered with golden roses. Even the thorns were like tiny golden needles.

Midas cocked his head at his wife. "What's wrong, my dear? Don't you see? Now we have the only gold roses in the world. Nobody else has them."

"Midas, the roses were beautiful just the way

73

they were," Queen Lydia said.

Midas scarcely heard her. "Oh, Lydia, with my new power, people will be talking about the great King Midas for centuries. This is the best thing that has ever happened to me!"

The queen was silent.

Midas's tail drooped. *Lydia doesn't seem as impressed as I thought she'd be. She must be overwhelmed by my wonderful power*, he decided.

"Come with me," Midas said. "Wait till you see what I've done to the palace."

Midas led his wife through the gardens and back inside. At the sight of the gold furnishings, the queen's mouth dropped open.

"Pretty nice, eh?" Midas said, his tail wagging proudly. "I'll bet you never thought you'd live in an all-gold palace."

Queen Lydia sighed. "No, I never did." She walked out of the room, shaking her head.

Midas hopped up on a chair to relax. The soft silk cushions instantly turned to solid gold at his touch.

"Ouch!" Midas cried as he thumped down on the rock-hard cushions. *Gold upholstery sure looks a lot better than it feels*, he thought.

Midas put his nose on his paws and did his best to make himself comfortable. *I must be the only king in the world with an all-gold couch*, he reminded himself. *At last I have the kind of power I've always dreamed of. In fact, this is better than my wildest dreams. I once wished to be a friend to the gods. But with power like this, I'm practically a god myself!*

74

Midas certainly is enjoying his wish. You might say it's all he can think about right now. He thinks his golden powers are the best thing in the world.

Joe has a lot to think about, too. He's the boss of his own business. But success can change your life . . . and not always for the better! Let's see how Joe is handling his new situation.

CHAPTER
10

Joe stood in front of his bedroom mirror. He studied his image as he knotted his dark blue necktie.

Wishbone looked up from where he lay on the bed. "Hey, buddy, are you sure you want to do that? That thing looks a lot like a leash to me. You'd better watch out someone doesn't tie you to a tree."

A shiny white dry-erase board was propped up on Joe's desk. Wishbone eyed it curiously. "That's my meeting Agenda," Joe explained, going over to the board. "Number one: Professionalism. Number two: Increasing client base. Number three: Productivity gains and goals."

Wow, Joe is sure using a lot of big words these days, Wishbone thought.

Joe kept reading and rehearsing. "Number four: Employee of the Week—Congratulations, David."

Wishbone snorted. "David? What about me? I work like a dog for this company, and what do I get?"

Wishbone cocked his ears. He heard two people coming up the stairs. A moment later, Sam and

David walked in. They seemed surprised by the sight of the dry-erase board and Joe in his tie.

Joe turned and nodded at them. "Oh, good. You're right on time for our business meeting. Punctuality is very important, you know."

David and Sam glanced at each other. David raised an eyebrow. A smile tugged at the corner of Sam's lips.

Joe gestured toward the bed. "Have a seat."

Silently, Sam and David sat down. Wishbone put his head in Sam's lap. Sam scratched behind Wishbone's ears, right in his favorite spot. Wishbone sighed happily. "Oh, Sam, keep that up, and you'll be Dog Scratcher of the Year," he said.

Joe cleared his throat. His face wore an unusually serious expression. "Attention, staff. I will now officially start the meeting."

Sam and David looked at each other again. David coughed to cover a laugh.

Joe picked up a long pointer from his desk. He rapped the tip of the pointer against the dry-erase board. "The first item on our agenda is professionalism."

Joe paused to straighten his tie. "As you know, we have more than thirty clients now. It's time to present a more professional face to them and all our potential clients, too. That's why I have pro-pro . . ." He paused a moment, trying to think of the word. " . . . procured new uniforms for us." He grinned. "We'll wear them when we shop and when we deliver. That way, everyone will recognize us as Joe's Grocery Delivery staff members."

Sam's mouth dropped open in surprise. "But, Joe, we agreed I would make the uniforms. Look, I brought the T-shirts." She unzipped her backpack and took out three large T-shirts. "I painted them myself."

Wishbone looked over. Each shirt was painted with different types of food—carrots, corn, and broccoli; bananas, apples, and pears; bread and muffins.

"Nice work, Sam," Wishbone said. "I like the food theme."

Sam pulled a fourth shirt from her backpack. It was much smaller than the others. It was covered with pictures of steaks, lamb chops, sausages, and drumsticks.

Sam grinned. "There's even one for Wishbone."

Wishbone lifted his head and cocked his ears. "For me? Yahoo!" He ran over to get a closer look. "Wow! Sausage! Chicken! Steak!" He pawed at the shirt, then looked up at Sam. "Hey, does this come in scratch-and-sniff?"

Joe shook his head. "They're cute, Sam, but they're just too homemade."

Sam frowned. "Joe, I spent a lot of time making these shirts."

"I'm sorry, Sam," Joe said firmly. "We need something more professional." He put down his pointer and headed toward his closet. "Here, look at these."

David and Sam stood up and followed Joe over to the closet.

With a flourish, Joe opened the closet door. He pulled out three matching uniforms on hangers. Each uniform had brown polyester pants and a tan shirt. There were also three matching brown caps.

Joe waved the uniforms, a big smile on his face.

"Aren't these great? I got them at a second-hand uniform store," he explained proudly. "They did the stitching, too."

He turned the shirts around to show Sam and David. Embroidered on the backs were the words *JOE'S GROCERY DELIVERY*. Stitched below that was the Talbots' phone number.

Sam and David regarded the uniforms doubtfully. "Uh, Joe, they look . . ." David began. His voice trailed off.

"You wouldn't believe how cheap they were," Joe went on enthusiastically. He handed Sam and David their uniforms. "You'll have them paid for in less than three hours of work."

Sam wrinkled her nose. "Joe, this thing smells as if it's been deep-fried."

David fingered his uniform and frowned. "It feels like it, too. I don't want to pay for this crummy uniform."

"Me either," said Sam. "It's not fair. I don't even like this thing."

Joe glared at them. "I don't care if you don't like them," he burst out angrily. "They're our uniforms."

He crossed to his desk and picked up a book called *So You Want to Be an Entrepreneur.* Joe flipped through the book until he found the page he wanted. "Listen to this. 'Uniforms can be an especially convincing way for young entrepreneurs to impress clients. Uniforms convey a sense of seriousness, professionalism, and dedication.'"

David and Sam just looked at each other. "What about a sense of fun?" Sam whispered. But Joe didn't seem to hear her.

Several days later, Wishbone stood outside the grocery store. He watched as Joe, David, and Sam loaded bag after bag of groceries into their carts. All three wore their tan and brown uniforms. Bicycle helmets covered their brown caps.

"Looks like a pretty good haul today," Wishbone said. "Just go ahead and put that bag of cold cuts right in my cart. I'll be sure to give it my personal attention."

Once the groceries were loaded, Wishbone hopped into his spot in the cart behind Joe's bike. Joe mounted the seat in front of him. "Ready, everyone? Let's go!"

Joe stood up and pushed down on his pedals. His bike started moving. The grocery cart rolled along behind it, picking up speed. Sam and David followed him down the tree-lined street.

Wishbone's ears flapped in the breeze. His tail wagged with excitement. His nose filled with the delicious smells of trees and grass.

"Yippee!" he cried. "Now this is what I call flying. By the way, will we be getting a meal on this flight?"

Sam pedaled alongside Joe's bike. Then she passed him.

A few moments later, David rode by, pedaling hard. He had a grin on his face.

"Hey, you guys, wait up!" Joe called after them.

Wishbone craned his neck to see in front of Joe. Up ahead, David and Sam were riding side by side now.

David turned to Sam. "Let's race!" he yelled.

"You're on!" Sam yelled back.

They both began pedaling harder. Their bikes moved faster and faster.

"Hey! What are you doing?" Joe called after them.

"They're having fun, Joe," Wishbone told him. "Come on! We can catch up."

"Be careful!" Joe yelled. "The groceries—"

But it was too late. Sam's bike hit a bump. It wobbled. She struggled to hang on.

"Uh-oh! Sam's in trouble!" Wishbone called.

Sam's bike swerved and she lost her balance. Her bicycle tipped over and she tumbled off sideways. "Ouch!" Sam yelled as she hit the ground.

The grocery cart came unhitched from Sam's bike and rolled toward the side of the road. Then it crashed into the curb and toppled. Bags flew out, spilling food everywhere.

"Oh, no! Wipeout!" Wishbone cried.

David slammed on the brakes and rushed to where Sam was sitting beside her fallen bicycle.

Joe pedaled his bike around the spilled food and skidded to a stop beside Sam and David. Sam was holding a banged-up elbow. Her uniform was shredded at the knee. An angry red scrape showed through the torn fabric.

"Sam, those are my profits!" Joe yelled, pointing at the spilled groceries. "That's good money you spilled all over the street!"

"Sam, are you okay?" David asked with concern. He helped Sam carefully to her feet. "Your leg is bleeding."

Sam glared at Joe. "I'm fine, David. It's nice to know someone around here cares about people, not money and profits!" She rubbed her elbow. "Joe, thanks a lot for being so concerned about me."

Joe sighed. "I'm sorry you got hurt, Sam," he said. "But it's your own fault. You shouldn't be playing on the job. You took a risk, and you're not the only one who's paying for it."

Sam and David stared at Joe. "I can't believe you!" Sam said angrily.

"You acted totally unprofessionally," Joe continued.

"That's it!" Sam exploded. Her green eyes flashed. "You don't care about anything but money anymore, Joe. We were trying to help you. Not because it was our job but because you're our friend. We thought it would be fun to do something together, but if this is the way you're going to act, forget it. I quit!"

She turned and walked back to her bike, limping slightly. David watched her for a moment, then looked back at Joe.

"She's right, Joe," David said. He shook his head. "I'm sorry. I quit too."

Without another word, Sam and David picked up their bikes. David unhitched his grocery cart. Then the two of them turned and walked their bikes away.

Joe stood in the street, staring after them in disbelief. Spilled groceries lay all around him.

"You can't do this!" Joe yelled. "You can't screw everything up and leave me holding the bag. You're not quitting. You're fired!"

Uh-oh. It looks as if Joe got his wish. But he

lost something precious at the same time. Meanwhile, Midas is having some trouble with his wish-come-true as well. Let's see what's going on back at the palace.

CHAPTER
11

With a flourish, Midas touched the clay bowl on the table in front of him. "Ta-dah!"

An awed gasp went up from the crowd of people watching as the clay bowl turned into gold.

"That's nothing," Midas said happily. "Watch this!" He trotted around the table and nosed another bowl. It, too, turned to gold. "And this!" He touched a goblet, transforming it into gold. "And this and this and this!" Midas raced around the table, touching everything in sight.

Midas stepped back, panting, and surveyed his work. "There you go. Gold place settings for eight. Not to mention gold napkins, gold candles, and gold place cards!"

An excited murmur went up from the group. It was early evening. Midas wanted to show off his new power, so he'd invited everyone he could think of to the palace for a demonstration. *I'm truly top dog now! By tomorrow, I won't be famous just in Phrygia. After this, the whole empire will be*

talking about me-the great King Midas!

Midas sat back and gazed around the room happily. The nobles of Phrygia stared in astonishment at the palace's new gold furnishings. They stroked the gold columns. They admired themselves in the golden plates.

In a corner, a group of musicians played. Wouldn't it be great if they were playing gold instruments? Midas thought.

Midas trotted over to the harp and placed his paw on it. Instantly, it was transformed entirely into shining gold.

"Oh!" cried the harp player in surprise.

"Okay, who's next?" Midas asked. But the other musicians grabbed their instruments and held them tightly.

"Excuse me, Your Highness, but—" the harpist began.

"There's no need to thank me," Midas said. "Nothing to it."

"Your Highness, this golden harp is very beautiful," the harpist said. "But there's a problem. The strings have been turned into solid gold. They won't make any sound. Can you please change the harp back to the way it was, so I can play it?"

"Uh, no, sorry, I can't," Midas admitted. "You see, this golden touch thing doesn't work in reverse. It's kind of a one-way street."

To take his mind off what had happened, Midas touched his nose to a bouquet of flowers on a nearby table. The flowers turned instantly to gold.

"Go on," he urged the guests. "Take a gold flower."

A woman in a green robe stepped forward and picked one of the blossoms. Light reflected off its golden petals. "It's beautiful, Your Highness," she whispered.

Midas's chest swelled with pride. "Think of it as a souvenir—a party favor," he told her. He held his head high. "I can turn anything into gold. Anything!"

Midas saw Queen Lydia entering the room. She smiled and then came toward him when he caught her eye.

"I have hardly seen you all day, my dear!" she said. "Every time I look for you, it seems you are turning something else into gold." A look of concern crossed her face. "Perhaps you should rest a while."

"I can't. The crowd loves my new power!" Midas wagged his tail happily. Suddenly he felt his stomach grumble. "I am hungry, though," he admitted. "I've been so busy turning things into gold, I forgot to eat!" He laughed. "That's never happened to me before."

Midas turned toward a table piled high with food. "Excuse me, everyone," he said. "I've got to take a break from using my golden powers. I'm afraid hunger calls. And when hunger calls, I'm always the first one to answer!"

A platter of freshly baked rolls sat near the edge of one of the golden tables. Midas reached out to take a roll in his mouth. But to his surprise, the soft bread turned hard at his touch.

Midas dropped the roll. It fell to the floor with a loud clatter. He stared down at it. "Why, it's solid gold!" he exclaimed.

He looked around at the shocked guests. "Ha-ha! Golden rolls. Will you look at that!" Midas tried to look pleased. "Who would like a special golden roll?"

The crowd began to murmur. A few people stepped back, looking worried.

"It's okay. There's nothing to worry about. I'll just have something else," Midas said quickly.

Midas sniffed at the food on the table. *Mmmm, cheese! That smells great!*

Midas leaned over the plate. He opened his mouth and prepared to sink his teeth into a soft wedge of cheese.

"Ouch!" he cried as the cheese turned hard and cold. He'd nearly broken a tooth on that one!

Midas saw the queen staring at him from the crowd of onlookers. She held one hand over her mouth. Her eyes were wide with dismay.

Help! I'm starving here! What am I going to do? Midas thought in a panic. *Okay, calm down. Think! Hey, maybe if I don't actually take the food myself, it won't turn into gold. Let's find out.*

Midas turned and saw a servant carrying a bowl filled with grapes. He beckoned the man over with a wave of his paw. "Come here. Feed me those grapes. Drop them into my mouth one by one."

The servant looked surprised, but he hurried to

obey. He broke off a grape and tossed it to the king. Midas caught the fruit easily in his mouth.

As soon as the grape touched his tongue, Midas felt the fruit change. It was no longer soft and juicy, but hard and cold. Midas coughed and sputtered. He struggled not to choke on the small golden nugget.

Finally, Midas managed to spit the grape out onto the floor. The gold grape rolled into a corner, where it clinked against the wall.

Another worried murmur went up from the crowd.

"Try again!" Midas commanded the servant.

Nervously, the young man broke off another grape. He tossed it to the king.

Once again, Midas had to spit out the gold grape. It dropped to the floor with a clatter.

Now the murmurs in the crowd turned to frightened gasps.

This can't be happening, Midas thought. *There must be something I can eat. Anything! Maybe I could have a drink.*

Frantic, Midas turned to the servant. "Find me a drink! Quickly!" he pleaded. He placed his front paws on the young man's leg. Midas felt the man's flesh turn hard and cold under his paws.

> Oh, no! Midas is completely unable to eat and drink! What a horrible fate!

"Oh, no!" he cried.

But it was too late. The servant stood before him, a statue of solid gold.

A terrified gasp went up from the crowd.

"I didn't mean it!" Midas said. "It was an accident!"

He took a step toward the nobles. But they all shrank back. Someone screamed. In a panic, the guests ran away from the king. There was a stampede toward the door.

"Wait! Where are you going?" Midas called after them. "Come back! Please! Everything will be all right!"

But in a matter of seconds, the room had emptied. Only King Midas and Queen Lydia remained among the gold furnishings.

King Midas took a step toward his wife. The queen let out a sob and ran from the room.

What have I done? Midas wondered. He lay down and put his paws sadly over his nose. *If I cannot eat, how can I live? And will I never again feel the touch of a human hand? Will I never again be able to hug my wife or kiss my daughter? Oh, what have I wished upon myself?*

It looks as if Midas's wish for the golden touch might not have been such a good idea after all. I guess Midas could have used a little boning up on his wishing technique!

Meanwhile, Joe's facing some problems of his own. Let's see how he's doing.

CHAPTER 12

Joe stood in the middle of the living room. In one hand, he held a bunch of bananas. In the other was a grocery list. A bag of frozen bagels was tucked under his arm. Groceries were all over the living room. Fruits and vegetables covered the coffee table. Boxes of cereal and pasta were stacked on the couch.

Joe looked from the list in his hand to the groceries, then back to the list again. His forehead was creased in concentration.

Wishbone sat on an overstuffed armchair in the corner. He could hardly believe his eyes. Look at all this food! If I'm dreaming, please don't wake me up.

He stood up. On the ottoman directly in front of him was another heap of groceries, with a carton of eggs at the top.

"Hey, Joe? You forgot the eggs," Wishbone said helpfully. He nosed at the carton. It fell to the floor. "Oops!"

Just then, the phone rang. Joe grabbed the receiver. "Hello? Oh, hi, Tim." A wistful look crossed his face. "Oh, that sounds great. I'd love to play basketball with you guys at the park. But there's no way. I've got so many groceries to deliver. . . . Yeah, maybe next time. Bye."

Joe replaced the receiver and sighed loudly. "Business comes first," he reminded himself.

"Right, buddy, I'm with you," Wishbone said. "I'll tell you what. Since Sam and David are gone, you deliver and I'll supervise."

Joe searched frantically around the room. "I know I bought hot dogs!" he wailed. He looked between the grocery bags, then under the coffee table. "Where are they?"

Joe grabbed a long, curled-up grocery receipt and unrolled it. He scanned the paper. "There! I did buy them!" He jabbed his finger at the receipt in triumph. Then he looked around the room. "So they've got to be here somewhere."

Wishbone felt the cold plastic package of hot dogs by one of his back legs. He nudged it quickly under a pillow then rolled on his back in front of it.

Joe continued searching. Then he glanced in Wishbone's direction. "Hey, Wishbone?"

Wishbone bolted upright. "What? I didn't do it! I was framed!"

"Wishbone, find the hot dogs!" Joe commanded.

Wishbone let out his breath. "Oh, sure. Put the dog to work." He lay back down. "Hmmph!"

Wishbone put his nose on his paws and watched Joe scurry around the room. Soon his eyelids grew heavy. Just watching Joe do all that work makes me tired, he thought. Well, according to my business plan, it is officially naptime.

Wishbone let out a long sigh and drifted off to sleep.

When Wishbone opened his eyes, the piles of groceries were gone from the floor, tables, and couch. In their place, a neat row of grocery bags stood on the floor near the coffee table.

Joe was sitting on the couch. He looked exhausted, his eyes at half-mast.

Wishbone jumped down to the floor. "Mmmm, what is that delicious aroma?" He began to sniff the grocery bags, following the scent.

As Wishbone rounded the back of the couch, he discovered an overturned carton. Beneath it was a pink, sticky puddle. He ran over and started licking. "Strawberry ice cream! It would be a shame to let all this go to waste," he said between slurps.

A few moments later, the Talbots' front door opened. Wishbone peered out from behind the couch as Ellen and Wanda walked in.

Ellen looked around the living room. Her eyes widened in surprise. "Joe! What's going on?" She checked her watch. "It's getting late. You're usually finished with your deliveries by now." Her forehead wrinkled with concern. "And you can't let fresh food sit out all afternoon. It could spoil, and then someone could get sick."

Wanda looked around the room at the bags of groceries. "Where are David and Sam?" she asked.

"You're not doing all this by yourself, are you?"

Joe sighed deeply. "It's a long story," he said quietly. He looked up at his mother and Wanda. "You haven't seen a carton of strawberry ice cream, have you? That's the only thing I can't find."

Wishbone burped. "Strawberry ice cream? Oops! I'll just pretend I didn't see it." He strolled casually toward the center of the living room. "Oh, hi, Ellen! How was your day at the library?"

Everyone stared at him.

"What?" Wishbone asked, looking around.

"Oh, no!" Joe moaned.

Wishbone turned to look over his shoulder. A trail of sticky pink paw prints led behind the couch.

Joe flung up his arms in exasperation. "I have to go to the grocery store again!" he cried. "This will be the third time today!"

Ellen shook her head sadly.

Wanda looked concerned. "Joe, do you need help?"

Ellen shot Wanda a quick, warning look and shook her head. "This is Joe's business, not ours, remember?" she said softly.

"I mean, I know a great courier service. They could deliver all this for you."

For the first time that day, Joe's face brightened. "That would be great!"

Wanda raised her eyebrows and looked apologetic. "They're kind of expensive, though."

Joe sighed. "I guess I don't have any choice," he said, shaking his head.

An hour later, Joe stood at the Talbots' front door. Wishbone watched as he handed the last of the grocery bags to the courier. Reaching into the large glass jar, Joe took out most of the bills. He handed over the money and closed the door.

Ellen walked in from the living room and stood beside her son. She looked at Joe with a sympathetic expression on her face. "Well, you did it," she said encouragingly. "Everything's going to be delivered."

"Yeah." Joe looked down at the jar sadly. "But most of my profits just went right out the door with that courier. I've been working for a month and all I have is twenty dollars." He picked up the jar and showed it to his mother. "Yeah, I sure did it all right." His voice was filled with disappointment.

Ellen folded her arms across her chest. "Look, Joe. Every business has its setbacks. But there are some losses that don't show up on the balance sheet." She put her hand on Joe's shoulder. "I think the important thing is for you and Sam and David to work out your problems so you can be friends again.

Wishbone sighed sadly. "Yeah," he added. "I miss Sam and David."

"I know." Joe shook his head sadly. "But I'm not sure we can."

"Joe, I guess sometimes you have to dig pretty deep for a solution," Wishbone said.

Joe is in a pretty tough situation. So is King

Midas. In fact, he almost gave up hope that his problems would ever be solved. There was only one thing he could think of to do.

CHAPTER
13

Midas tossed and turned on his rock-hard gold bed. His empty stomach grumbled. "Oh, what I wouldn't do for a simple straw mat and a hunk of bread!" Midas moaned. "If only Bacchus would come back and let me have another wish. Then I could wish my first wish away." He thought a moment. "Or maybe I could just get rid of the part about eating and turning people into gold statues. The rest of the golden touch is pretty cool."

Then Midas had an idea. *Wait a minute! Maybe there is a way to change my wish. I'll ask one of the other gods for help. A food god, perhaps.*

Midas knew that not too far away there was a shrine to Demeter. She was the goddess of the harvest and the giver of grain and fruit. *Too bad there isn't a god of steaks and sausages,* Midas thought with a smile.

Midas jumped to his feet. He knew that there was an oracle, or priestess, at Demeter's shrine. That oracle spoke for the goddess. Maybe she

Many ancient Greeks visited oracles. They believed that the oracles were in direct contact with the god or goddess they represented. People would ask the oracle for advice or for favors. They thought the oracle could speak directly to her god or goddess and help grant the person's wish. So Midas's idea to visit Demeter's oracle was pretty sensible!

could help cure Midas of his wish.

The following day, Midas arrived in front of the great temple of Demeter. He was traveling alone. He had no choice. All of the palace servants were too frightened to go anywhere near him.

Midas wore sandals. Gold sandals, of course. They kept his paws from touching the ground and turning it into gold. The sandals rubbed uncomfortably against his paws. His legs were sore and dusty from the long walk, and they ached from the weight of the gold sandals. He still wore the heavy gold hat to cover his donkey ears. His stomach ached from hunger and his mouth was dry with thirst. *I've never felt so miserable in my whole life,* the king thought.

Midas stared up at the enormous stone temple in front of him. It was decorated with carvings of ears of corn and sheaves of wheat to honor the goddess. The carvings reminded Midas of the food he had turned into gold—food he could no longer eat.

A long line of visitors stood outside the temple. Midas joined the line, being careful not to touch anything or anyone. *I definitely can't reveal my power here*, he thought. *Everyone would be terrified and run away. Although that would shorten the line!*

A man stepped into line behind Midas. He wore the white tunic and metal helmet of an officer in the Greek navy.

"Good day, sailor," Midas greeted him. "What brings you to see the oracle?"

"I came to ask the goddess to bless our journey. My men and I are on our way home. What brings you here, fellow traveler?"

What can I say? Midas wondered. *That I'm trying to break a bad habit of turning people into gold statues? I don't think so.* "Oh, it's just a little . . . uh . . . problem I'm having," he said quickly.

"Where are you from?" the sailor asked.

"Phrygia," Midas replied. "Actually, I'm the king of Phrygia," he added proudly.

"Really? We sailed through Phrygia on the Pyrite River." The man stopped and stared. "Wait a minute! Are you King Midas?"

"That's right." Midas puffed out his chest. "No doubt you've heard of me."

The man burst out laughing. "I certainly have!" he exclaimed between guffaws. "There is a lot of

talk about you. Especially down by the river."

"Oh, you must have heard one of my jokes from the fishermen," Midas said. "They certainly seem to think I'm very funny."

But the sailor was now laughing too hard to talk.

Then Midas noticed that it was finally his turn to visit the oracle. He said good-bye to the laughing sailor and climbed the stone steps to the temple.

Midas trotted into the cool darkness of the temple. The oracle was seated against the far wall. She was dressed in robes of deep green and wore a green veil on her head. Her eyes were closed and her hands rested lightly on her lap. Behind her, a small flame burned in a hollowed-out spot in the wall. The flame cast flickering shadows around the room.

Ooh, it's kind of creepy in here, Midas thought

101

with a shiver. He cleared his throat. "Excuse me. Is this the complaint department?"

The priestess did not answer.

Midas tried again. "Hellooo! Can you help me? I need to talk to the goddess Demeter. It's very important. You see, I made a wish, and now I need to unmake it."

"Tell me the wish," the oracle commanded.

"Well, it all started when Bacchus granted me one wish," Midas began. "So I wished for the golden touch. I wanted everything I touched to turn to gold. And it worked! It was great at first. But now I can't eat because all my food turns to gold. And I can't touch anyone without turning him or her into gold. So . . . I'd like to take back my wish."

The priestess shook her head. "I'm sorry. I cannot help you."

The fur on the back of Midas's neck bristled. "Why not? Do the gods have some kind of 'no refunds, no exchanges' policy? There must be some kind of cure!"

When the oracle spoke again, Midas could barely hear her. "Yes, there is."

Midas cocked his ears. His tail wagged in excitement. "What is it? Tell me!"

"You alone have the answer," the oracle said. Her voice echoed softly in the temple. "You will know it when you are ready."

"I'm ready! I'm ready!"

The priestess shook her head slowly. "No. You cannot be ready while even a speck of your heart longs for gold."

"Oh, come on! Can't you just give me a hint? A teeny, tiny, little hint?" Midas begged.

But the oracle was silent.

"Okay, well, thanks anyway, I guess," Midas said. His tail drooped. He nosed some rocks, turning them into gold nuggets. "Here. This should settle my bill."

Without opening her eyes, the oracle shook her head. "Worthless," she said.

"Worthless?" Midas couldn't believe his ears. "These are solid gold. They're worth a fortune!"

But the oracle just shook her head again.

Disappointed, Midas turned to leave. As he did, his tail brushed against a column. Immediately, it turned to solid gold.

Nothing has changed, the king thought. His stomach growled again. *I came all this way, and I've still got the golden touch. What in the world can I do now?*

Midas made his slow, sad way home. When he finally arrived back at the palace he was hungry, tired, and disappointed. He trudged down the golden floor of the hallway. The queen was waiting for him in the palace's main chamber.

"Midas!" she cried, her face full of hope. "Did you have any luck?"

Midas shook his head. "No. The golden touch is still with me."

The queen's face fell. "What did the oracle say?" she asked. "Is there no cure?"

"Oh, there's a cure all right," Midas replied. He jumped up on one of the gold chairs. "But the oracle won't tell me what it is."

The queen frowned. "Why on earth not?"

"She said it would be revealed to me when I was ready." Midas sighed. "Whatever that means."

"I suppose we must be patient, then," Lydia replied.

"Patient? How can I be patient?" Midas cried. "I'm so hungry! And so tired!" He put his nose down on his paws. "I am almost ready to give up hope."

"Try to rest, my dear," Lydia said gently.

Midas closed his eyes. Lydia began to sing a soothing melody. *How I long for the touch of her hand,* Midas thought sadly. *And how I wish I could kiss my daughter's sweet face again!*

Despite his sadness, Midas felt himself begin to relax. He took a deep breath. The queen's soft melody filled his ears. He began to drift off to sleep.

Suddenly, Midas heard small feet running toward him. *Ah, that must be Ariel,* he thought sleepily. *Then he opened his eyes with a start. Ariel? Oh, no!*

But it was too late. His daughter was running straight toward him.

"Hi, Daddy!" she cried. "Where have you been?" Her beautiful face shone with excitement. She ran toward Midas, her hands outstretched.

The queen jumped to her feet. "Ariel, no!" she cried.

She grabbed for her daughter's arm, but it was too late. Together their hands brushed against Midas.

Suddenly, the room was deathly quiet.

Midas stared in horror. His wife and daughter stood before him. They had both been turned to solid gold, frozen forever into still, silent statues.

Ariel still had her sweet smile. Lydia's face wore a shocked expression.

Midas felt terror grip his body from nose to tail. "What have I done?" he cried. "Oh, what have I done?" He felt as if his heart had been torn from his chest.

Oh, no! Turning his wife and daughter into gold was even worse than not being able to eat! It looks as if wishes don't always turn out the way you plan them. Take Joe, for instance. He's finding out that the successful business he wished for may not be a dream come true after all.

CHAPTER
14

Wishbone sat on the floor of Joe's room. Joe sat beside him. He looked grim.

"Forget it," Joe said, shaking his head. "There's no way I can do all this by myself." He looked at the list in his hand. "Thirty orders." He shook his head again.

"Wait a minute," Joe said after thinking for a moment. "Maybe I could pick up the shopping lists after school on Tuesday and Wednesday."

"Sounds good to me," Wishbone said.

"That leaves Thursday, Friday, and Saturday for shopping and deliveries," Joe continued. "The grocery store is open all night. If I woke up at five o'clock every day—"

"Ooh," Wishbone groaned. "Five o'clock is way too early for the dog." He put his head down on his paws.

But Joe looked determined. He stood up and reached for the alarm clock on his night-table.

"I guess it's the only way," he muttered.

The next morning, Wishbone was awakened by a loud noise.

"What's that?" Wishbone jumped to his feet and shook himself vigorously. Beside him on the bed, Joe groaned and rolled over.

The alarm clock on the bed rang noisily. The clock read 5:00.

Sleepily, Joe reached for the alarm and turned it off. He rubbed his eyes and yawned.

"Let's go, Joe! Move it, move it!" Wishbone ordered in his best army drill-sergeant's voice.

Joe struggled to sit up. He rubbed his eyes again. He sat on the edge of his bed as if in a trance. Finally, he managed to stagger to his feet.

The moment Joe was out of bed, Wishbone flopped back down in the warm spot Joe had left. "Mmmm," Wishbone sighed, snuggling down into the covers. "I never said I was a morning person." He started to drift back to sleep.

Joe's voice woke him a few minutes later. "Come on, Wishbone. We've got shopping to do and deliveries to make."

"Oh, all right," Wishbone said with a yawn. "You can always count on the faithful dog."

Wishbone jumped down and trotted downstairs. He followed Joe outside and took his place in the back of the grocery cart.

The sun was just beginning to rise as Joe pedaled out of the driveway.

Two hours later, Joe had shopped for and sorted three orders. The grocery cart was filled.

Wishbone trotted alongside.

They arrived at the first house. Joe parked his bike and lifted two grocery bags out of the cart. Wishbone followed him up the walkway to the house. All the windows in the house were dark.

Joe rang the doorbell. Nothing happened.

Joe rang the bell again. He waited.

Finally, the door opened. An older woman wearing a bathrobe and hair curlers stood there, rubbing her eyes sleepily.

"Joe's Grocery Delivery at your service," Joe said brightly. He handed her the bags.

"Kind of early, aren't you?" the woman mumbled. Then she yawned and went back into the house, closing the door behind her.

Joe and Wishbone went back to the bike. "That's one down," Joe said. "Only two more this morning—and about a zillion more later on. Come on, Wishbone. We've got a lot of work to do."

Finally, they finished their deliveries. When they got back to the Talbots' house, Wishbone ran straight over to his big red chair. Joe flopped down on the couch with an exhausted sigh.

Ellen walked into the living room. "Joe, you'd better get moving," she said. "You don't want to be late for school."

"School! I forgot about school." Joe shook his head. "How am I ever going to make it through a full day of school after all that work?"

Wishbone put his nose on his paws. "You can do it, Joe. I'll be right here when you get home."

That night, Ellen walked upstairs to check on Joe. He had been working on his homework for a long time. Ellen hoped he wouldn't be up too late trying to catch up.

Ellen pushed open Joe's bedroom door. "Joe?" she called softly.

Joe was at his desk. His math book was open in front of him. His head was resting on the open book. His eyes were closed, and a pencil dangled loosely from one hand. He was sound asleep.

Ellen smiled sympathetically. "Poor Joe," she whispered. "He's certainly paying the price for putting his business first."

Then Ellen glanced down at Joe's feet. Curled up on the rug at the foot of the chair was Wishbone. He was fast asleep, too.

On Friday evening, Joe and Wishbone sat on the living room couch. Wishbone sighed.

It's been one tough week, Wishbone thought. *Shopping, sorting, delivering. I've barely had any time to take care of my real business. You know— chewing, digging, and burying. I'm even neglecting Wanda's garden!*

A stack of books was piled high on the coffee table in front of Joe. One by one, Joe opened the books and scanned their indexes.

"What are you trying to find, Joe?" Wishbone asked.

Joe shook his head. "It's not in here," he muttered. Just then, Ellen walked into the room. "What are you looking for?" she asked.

Joe looked up from the book. "I was just . . . oh, never mind." He tossed the book on the coffee table. "It sounds stupid."

Ellen smiled and sat down next to him. "Tell me, Joe. I promise not to make fun of you," she said.

"Well, I wanted to find out whether any of these books said anything about friends," Joe admitted. "I wondered if an entrepreneur could . . . you know . . . have some."

"I see." Ellen nodded. "I don't think you'll find very much about friendship in these books, Joe. But it sure would be nice to have your friends' help, wouldn't it?"

"Yeah, but they just don't get it!" Joe sounded exasperated.

"Get what?" Ellen asked.

"They don't understand that this business is mine. I own it. I built it. I want to work. But all they want to do is play."

"Well, maybe work and play don't have to be so different," Ellen suggested. "When you play basketball, is that work or play?"

Joe thought for a moment. "It's both," he said at last. "It's fun, but everyone on the team has to work together to win the game."

"Maybe that's what Sam and David wanted—to be part of a team," Ellen said. "They wanted to get excited and pull together to accomplish something. And they wanted to have some fun, too."

Ellen handed Joe a book. "Here. I picked this up for you at the library. I got it because I know you've always been a team player at heart."

Wishbone looked at the book as Joe read the title: *"Teamwork: The Spirit of Success."*

Joe studied the book's cover for a moment, thinking. Then he grinned. "You're right. If a guy on our team acted the way I did, he'd be on the bench for the whole season. Coach Menendez always says, 'Don't be a selfish player.' I guess I've been acting pretty selfish lately."

Ellen smiled and put her arm around Joe's shoulder.

"Thanks, Mom," Joe said. He got to his feet. Wishbone looked up expectantly. "I've got a couple of phone calls to make."

I think Joe is finally figuring out the right thing to do. Okay, so maybe it took a while, but at least he came to his senses. Let's see if King Midas has come to his senses yet.

CHAPTER 15

Midas sat miserably beside the silent gold statues of his wife and daughter. Mournfully, he kissed Ariel's hand. *Oh, please, change back!* he wished. But the gold stayed hard and cold.

"I curse my own greed!" Midas howled. "Now I only wish never to see gold anywhere again! I would do anything, anything to change this foolish wish!"

Suddenly the room was filled with purple smoke. When the cloud cleared, Bacchus appeared. He held a goblet in one hand and a hunk of bread in the other.

Midas sat up. His tail began to wag. "Bacchus!" he said eagerly. "Am I glad to see you!"

"Well, it's about time," Bacchus snapped impatiently. "I was wondering how long it would take you to unwish your foolishness."

"Oh, I do, I do!" Midas replied.

"All right, then. Let's take care of this so I can get back to my party," Bacchus grumbled.

Midas jumped up onto all fours. "You mean you

can do it? You can remove the curse?"

"Yes, now that you finally realize you cursed yourself by wishing for wealth above all else." Bacchus popped the last of his bread into his mouth and snapped his fingers. Instantly, a bundle of scrolls appeared in his hand.

"This is the *Encyclopedia of Wishes*," Bacchus explained. He searched through the scrolls. "Let's see . . . gold . . . gold coins . . . golden eggs . . . ah! Here it is. The golden touch."

Bacchus studied the scroll for a moment. Then he turned to Midas. "You must bathe yourself in the falls of the Pyrite River. Then your wish will wash away."

"No problem!" Midas agreed happily. Normally he hated baths. But to get his family back, he would do absolutely anything.

"What about my wife and daughter? Will all be as it was?" he asked anxiously.

Bacchus nodded. "You must first touch everything else you turned into gold. It will all be restored to its original state. But you can't hope to keep some of the gold. You must touch every single candlestick, every lump of dirt. Only then will you be able to free your family. Remember, touch everything."

Midas nodded. "Everything. I've got it. Thank you, O divine one. I will never make a mistake like this again."

"You'd better not." Bacchus stared at him. "By the way, what's with the party hat?"

Midas touched a paw to the huge hat on his

head. "Don't ask," he replied shamefully. His tail drooped. "It's just more of my own foolishness."

With a shrug, Bacchus disappeared in a cloud of purple smoke.

The moment the god was gone, Midas raced out of the palace. He hurried through the countryside toward the river as fast as his four legs would carry him.

When Midas got to the riverbank, he stopped. A strange sound was coming from the tall reeds by the river's edge.

"What's that?" Midas cocked his ears.

The wind blew, and the sound began again.

"Oh, it's just the wind making the reeds rustle," Midas said. "But it sounds like . . . like words!"

Indeed, a whispering sound came from the reeds. Midas cocked his ears. He stepped closer and listened.

"King Midas has donkey's ears . . . King Midas has donkey's ears . . ." the reeds murmured. The voice sounded strangely familiar.

"That's Phidias's voice!" Midas said in surprise. He peered into the reeds, looking for his royal hairdresser. "Phidias, are you in there?"

"King Midas has donkey's ears . . . King Midas has donkey's ears," the reeds whispered again. But no one was there. And Midas's keen nose could pick up no scent other than the grass and water.

"What's going on?" Midas asked out loud.

Just then, Midas saw Phidias himself coming down the road. "Phidias, what's going on?" the king yelled.

"Wh-what do you mean?" the royal hairdresser asked nervously.

"I was walking along the road when I suddenly heard a voice saying, 'King Midas has donkey's ears' over and over. And the voice was yours! Have you been hiding in the reeds, telling people my secret?"

"No, Your Highness!" Phidias cried. "I promised you I would not breathe a word to another human soul."

"Then how do you explain that voice? Listen!" King Midas commanded.

Sure enough, the strange sound continued: "King Midas has donkey's ears . . . King Midas has donkey's ears."

"That's your voice! Besides, no one else knows about this. You must have broken your promise!"

> **Phidias buried his secret in a hole! What a great idea! I say there's nothing more satisfying than some good digging.**

Phidias's face flushed. "No, Your Highness. I did not tell another living soul, just as I promised. But I couldn't bear keeping the secret to myself. So I ran to the bank of the river and dug a hole. Then I spoke the secret into the earth."

"Then what happened?" Midas asked.

"Those reeds grew up from the hole that I dug," Phidias explained. "It is the reeds themselves who are whispering your secret to the world." Phidias looked down, embarrassed. "I'm sorry, Your Highness."

Midas thought about Phidias's story. *Phidias shared my secret with the ground, and those reeds sprang up. They've been whispering my secret ever since! No wonder the fishermen have been laughing at me! And that sailor at Demeter's shrine said he had sailed on this river. He must have heard the reeds gossiping about me, too!*

But Midas didn't care about his ears anymore. He had more important things to worry about. "Oh, never mind, Phidias, " he told the hairdresser. "I know you didn't mean any harm. Go on your way." Midas shook his head and watched the royal hairdresser continue his journey down the road. Then he resumed his own journey.

Midas hurried to the edge of the falls. He pushed off his hat. Then he put one paw in the water, then another. "Brrr! It's freezing in here! But at least it isn't turning to gold!"

Midas waded fully into the river and dog-paddled over to the falls. Then he stood beneath the falling water, feeling it drench his fur. He looked down. The sand beneath his paws was turning to gold as the water washed over him.

"Yes, yes! Wash away, golden touch!" he cried. He pranced in the water, splashing and yelling with delight. This time, he was happy to see something turning to gold. This time, it meant his golden touch was washing into the river.

There's an old Greek myth, or story, about Midas washing his golden touch into the sand. The myth explains why the sand in the Pyrite River looked like gold, even though there was no gold there. The real reason that the sands of the Pyrite River look like gold is that they are full of a shiny golden mineral. Today, the mineral gets its name from the river. It's called "pyrite."

Pyrite isn't made of gold at all, and it has no value. There's another name for pyrite. It's called "fool's gold" because anyone who thinks it is real gold is ... well ... a fool!

117

Finally Midas waded back to shore. He stepped onto the grassy riverbank and shook himself off vigorously.

"All right. The grass hasn't turned to gold. Now let's try another little experiment," Midas said. He took a deep breath and headed for a tree. Nervously, he touched his nose to the tree's trunk.

Nothing happened. To his relief, the trunk remained brown and gnarled. Its green leaves swayed gently in the breeze.

"It's gone! It's gone! The golden touch is gone!" Midas leaped into the air and did several flips. "Yippee!"

As Midas leaped, he saw his golden hat and golden sandals in the grass. He touched them quickly and the gold disappeared. He started to put his hat back on his head, but then he stopped. "Oh, who cares? Let the world see my ears if they must. I know what's truly important now," he said.

Leaving his hat in the grass, Midas bounded up the riverbank. I feel like a puppy again! he thought joyfully.

Midas raced back to the palace. He ran straight in the front door. His paws skidded as he rounded the corners. He hardly noticed the floor turning from gold into stone under his feet.

As quickly as he could, Midas ran around the room. He nosed the gold tables and the gold tapestries. He placed his paws on the gold rugs and the gold columns. His tail wagged happily as the objects transformed back into ordinary furnishings.

"I never thought I'd be so happy to see my gold disappear!" Midas said as he raced out to the garden to touch the gold out there.

Finally, he was done. Midas looked around in satisfaction. Every last thing had been restored to its natural state. Now he could free his family.

Midas went to stand before the statues of his wife and daughter. Standing up on his hind legs, he covered Lydia and Ariel with kisses.

At his touch, they sprang back to life.

The queen broke into a huge smile. "Midas! You did it! Oh, this is the happiest moment of my life!"

"And mine too!" Midas replied.

Ariel burst into giggles. She pointed at Midas's head. "Daddy, look at your ears! You look like a funny old donkey!"

Midas laughed with her. "Don't I, though? Hee-haw, hee-haw!" He brayed like a donkey, then laughed again. *I don't care one bit about my ears anymore*, he thought. *I'm just so grateful to have my family back again!*

"Oh, Daddy," Ariel said. She reached for Midas's ears. Tenderly, she kissed each of them.

Midas felt a soft tingling sensation at the spot of each of Ariel's kisses. Suddenly his head felt lighter. He raised a paw to his head and felt two small, soft triangles of fur.

They're gone! he realized in amazement. *Somehow, magically, through the power of my daughter's kiss, my ears have changed back to their original form!*

Midas looked at the happy faces of his wife and daughter. "Now I know that all the wealth and fame in the world are no guarantee of happiness," he told them. Midas was thankful—and very sorry for all he had done. "Gold could never replace the two of you," he said at last. "Now let's eat! I'm starving!"

So Midas finally got his happy ending. He had to give up his gold, but he got back the people who were the most important to him. And he learned an important lesson about what's really significant in life.

Meanwhile, Joe is trying to sort out what's important to him. Let's see what he's decided.

CHAPTER
16

Wishbone sat on Joe's bed. He heard familiar footsteps coming up the stairs.

"Joe!" he announced happily. "We've got visitors."

There was a knock on the bedroom door. "Come in," Joe called.

The door swung open. Sam and David stood in the doorway. They held their folded brown and tan uniforms in their hands.

"Sam! David! You're back!" Wishbone cried happily.

"Hi, Joe," Sam said quietly. "Why did you call us and ask us to come over?"

"And why did you tell us to bring these stupid uniforms?" David asked.

"Hi, guys," Joe said. A huge grin spread across his face. "I asked you to bring the uniforms back because Joe's Grocery Delivery is officially out of business."

Joe reached for the uniforms. "Here, let me take those." He tossed them into a large cardboard box

121

on the bed. "Ugh. I can't believe I made you guys wear those ugly things."

Wishbone sniffed the box. "I'd offer to bury them for you, pal, but I'm afraid they might be considered toxic waste."

"What a relief!" Joe said, sitting down on his bed. "I am done with this business. No more groceries, no more couriers, no more deliveries. I don't care if I never see another bag of groceries in my life!"

"Hey, I wouldn't go that far," Wishbone said.

"So, what are you going to do now?" Sam asked.

"I'm going to play basketball and stay caught up on my schoolwork," Joe said. His expression turned serious. "And I'm going to have fun with you guys. I'm really sorry about the way I've been acting. I know I've been a real jerk lately."

"You can say that again!" Sam agreed with a laugh.

"This business was really important to me," Joe admitted. "Too important. I thought making money would be the greatest thing in the world, but it's not. There's nothing more important than having a good time with my friends."

"All right, Joe!" David cheered.

"That's great!" Sam said. "We're glad to have the old Joe back again."

Joe walked over to his desk and picked up the profits jar. "I had to use a courier service to help me finish this week's orders, so this is all the money I have left. It's not much," he said as he fished out the two remaining ten-dollar bills. "But I want you guys to have this." He handed one bill to David and the other to Sam.

Sam and David smiled.

"What about me?" Wishbone reminded them. "I'll take my pay in steak, if that's all right."

"Hey, Joe, you know what?" David asked. "I think we have enough money to take you out to Pepper Pete's for a going-out-of-business party."

"That sounds great!" Joe agreed.

The three friends laughed and headed toward the door.

"You kids run along," Wishbone called after them. "Have a good time!" He watched them head out into the hall. He waited, listening, as they ran down the stairs.

"Okay, the coast is clear!" Wishbone announced when the house was quiet again. He jumped down, then crawled under Joe's bed. He quickly emerged, carrying the package of hot dogs that had been hidden there.

"I'll just stay here and inventory the leftovers," Wishbone said as he settled down on the rug with his snack. "Hmmm . . . I should have remembered to save some mustard."

About Ovid

O vid was a famous Roman poet. He was born in 43 B.C. in Sulmo, Italy. When his older brother died, his family put all their hopes on Ovid. They wanted him to be a big success.

Ovid went to Rome to study with the best teachers of law and logic. He became a lawyer and government official. He was well on his way to becoming a Roman senator when he decided to give up his career and devote his life to writing poetry instead. His poetry was very popular, both while he was alive and for centuries after he died.

In A.D. 8 Ovid was exiled to Tomi, which is now part of Romania. Nobody knows why he was exiled, but Ovid always denied he did anything wrong. He continued to write during his exile. He died in Tomi in A.D. 17 or 18.

Ovid wrote love poetry and at least one play. But his most famous work was *Metamorphoses*. This collection of 250 myths includes the story of King Midas. All the myths involve characters undergoing some type of change or metamorphosis. The stories include lots of gods, heroes and adventures. *Metamorphoses* has been called one of the greatest influences on Western literature and art. Great writers such as Shakespeare, Chaucer, Dante, and Milton based many of their stories on these myths first collected by Ovid.

HEY
GANG!

Wishbone here. If you enjoyed my adventures as King Midas, you'll love my next escapade in the Carpathian Mountains of Transylvania. You guessed it! I'm off to meet one of the scariest characters to swoop down from the skies, Count Dracula.

Here's a sneak preview . . .

COMING
SOON

The Adventures of **WISHBONE**™
Scent of a Vampire

Wishbone shut his eyes, imagining himself back in 1897, the year Bram Stoker published his classic tale, *Dracula*. The book was written as excerpts from diaries, journals, letters, and newspaper articles. This style made the book seem very realistic, as if the characters had left behind a record of their terrifying experiences.

Wishbone identified with Jonathan Barker—er, Harker—an eager pup of a lawyer, on his very first important assignment. Jonathan was handling the real estate deals of Count Dracula, a wealthy Transylvanian aristocrat. Wishbone pictured himself in Jonathan's proper suit, ideal for a young English attorney wanting to make a good impression. Jonathan thought this journey would mark the beginning of his new career. He had no idea how it would change his life.

May 3 Budapest

*I am keeping this journal so that I won't forget
a single detail of this marvelous trip. I want to
remember everything so I will be able to
describe all of my experiences to my beloved
Mina when I return home. (NOTE: Be sure to
get the recipe for last night's dinner of chicken
paprika for Mina.)*

*I am now traveling into the Carpathian
Mountains to Count Dracula's castle. The area
is one of the wildest and least known portions of
Europe. I read that it is also the home of all
sorts of superstitions. If so, my visit should
prove very interesting. (NOTE: I must ask
Count Dracula all about this.)*

"Whoa!" A sharp bump in the road sent the
pencil flying from Jonathan's mouth. His journal
slipped out from under his paws and fell to the
floor of the carriage.

Jonathan leaned down from the seat to retrieve
the journal. As he did, one of his fellow passengers
reached down too. The gentleman picked up the
journal and held it out to Jonathan.

"Thank you," Jonathan said.

The man smiled—until he glanced down at the
open page. His smile faltered and Jonathan saw
fear come into the man's eyes.

"Is there something wrong with my handwrit-
ing?" Jonathan asked. *Hey,* he thought, *it's tough
to write neatly with a pencil in your mouth*

in such a bumpy carriage.

The man touched the page gingerly. "Dracula?" he asked, pointing to the name Jonathan had written in the journal.

"Yes," Jonathan replied. "Do you know him?" He'd love to have a chance to talk to one of the count's countrymen. Jonathan was a little nervous about meeting someone of Count Dracula's stature. The count was very wealthy, with an impressive pedigree. And the customs of this country were different from England. Jonathan didn't want the count to think he was an ill-mannered mutt.

The man didn't answer Jonathan's question. He simply held out the journal. He lowered his eyes as if he couldn't bring himself to meet Jonathan's gaze.

Jonathan took the book in his mouth and placed it beside him on the carriage seat. Perhaps he doesn't understand English, Jonathan realized. He hadn't heard a single word of his own language since his arrival.

"Dracula," the man repeated in a low tone. He pulled a small pouch from his pocket.

Jonathan's nose wrinkled. *Is that garlic?* he wondered.

The man held out the pouch to Jonathan, waving it under Jonathan's muzzle.

"For me?" Jonathan said. "Uh, thanks. I prefer my garlic cooked. Preferably in spaghetti sauce."

The man continued to hold out the stinky pouch. "Dracula," the man said again, louder.

The woman sitting next to the man gasped. Her hands flew up and she hurriedly made the sign of the cross. The four other passengers began whispering. Jonathan could only make out a few words. The name "Dracula," of course. But his sharp ears also picked up the word for "vampire." At least, he thought that's what they were saying. Jonathan wasn't very sure of the language.

Jonathan had read about the strange creature known as the vampire. It figured prominently in the many superstitions of this country. It was believed that the vampire was an evil being who lived on the blood of others.

I'll have to remember to ask Count Dracula about this belief in vampires, Jonathan told himself.

One by one, the passengers were dropped off at their destinations. Jonathan wondered how far it was to the Borgo Pass. That was where Dracula had instructed him to wait. The count would send his own coach to take Jonathan the rest of the way.

on the maps he consulted back in London. It had been the site of terrible, bloody battles over the centuries, many of them fought and won by Dracula's ancestors. But he'd been unable to locate Dracula's castle, or even the county in which it was situated. The country was still fairly unexplored.

Jonathan sat across from an elderly lady—the last passenger aboard the carriage with him. She wore the traditional costume of the country. Her white underdress had full white sleeves, and the double-apron had elaborate embroidered designs.

She kept her head bowed and murmured what sounded to Jonathan like a prayer. He noticed she peeked at him every now and then, a worried expression on her face.

The coach rattled along the rugged road. Jonathan realized that now that the sun had gone down, the driver had dramatically picked up speed. Jonathan and the woman slid back and forth on the seats as the carriage rounded sharp curves at top speed. Finally, the driver came to a stop.

The woman leaned toward Jonathan. "Oh sir, I beg you," she whispered. "Please don't go to Dracula's castle.

"Wh-what?" Jonathan stared at her. He didn't know if he was more surprised by her words or by the fact that she spoke English. She had a thick accent but there was no mistaking what she said.

She grabbed his paw and held it in both of her hands. "Do you know where you're going? What you are going to?"

"I—Well, I have a vague notion," Jonathan replied. "I gather it's not exactly a prime tourist attraction."

The woman released his paw and shuddered. "Reconsider, please," she begged.

Jonathan judged the woman to be one of the more superstitious types. She wore a number of old-fashioned amulets. Guards against imaginary demons, Jonathan figured.

He knew she was only trying to be kind, so he did his best to calm her. He patted her arm with his paw. "It's perfectly safe," he told her. "I'm here on important business—that's all."

She rattled off something in a language Jonathan didn't understand. She still seemed upset as the driver opened the door and held out his hand to her. She quickly took off the chain she wore and slid it over Jonathan's ears, draping it over his neck. A fancy gold cross dangled from it.

Jonathan looked up, confused.

"Please, sir. Take it," she insisted. "If not for yourself, then for those who love you."

Before he could try to give the pendant back to her, the driver helped her out of the carriage. Moments later, the driver gave a sharp snap of his whip and started up the horses again.

Jonathan was now alone in the carriage. He didn't know if it was the old lady's fear, or the ghostly traditions of this strange country, but he felt uneasy.

The road was rough and uneven, but the carriage flew over it with a feverish haste. Jonathan could hear the driver cracking his whip, urging the horses to go faster—faster!

What's the hurry? Jonathan wondered. I guess the driver isn't worried about getting a speeding ticket in this desolate area.

The coach rocked and swayed like a boat being tossed by a stormy sea. *I never thought I'd have to worry about seasickness traveling overland*, Jonathan thought. He slipped off the seat again.

Fine, thought Jonathan. *If that's the way it's going*

to be. He curled up on the floor of the carriage, laying his muzzle across his front legs. *I'll stay down here where I'm less likely to be hurt*, he decided. *I'm tired of being tossed like a salad.*

Jonathan gazed up at the sky through the window. He could just make out the snowy peaks of the high cliffs above him. Dark clouds rolled across the high full moon. Distant thunder rumbled, leaving Jonathan to wonder if a storm was brewing.

"Are we there yet?" Jonathan called out. He didn't expect an answer. He knew the driver could not hear him seated atop the coach.

Soon the coach came to a stop.

Jonathan stood up on his hind legs and placed his front paws on the window of the carriage. He peered into the darkness, searching for the lamps of Count Dracula's carriage. But the only lights were the flickering lanterns at the front of the coach he was in.

The door to the coach opened. "It is nearly midnight," the driver said. "There is no carriage waiting for you. There must have been some mistake. Let us go back now and try again another day."

Before Jonathan could protest, the horses began to neigh and snort. The driver raced forward to grab their reins to keep them from charging. One of the horses reared up, sending Jonathan tumbling back onto the floor of the coach.

He scrambled back up to his four paws. He raised onto his hind legs again and poked his muzzle out the window.

A fancy two-seated coach drawn by four huge black stallions thundered out of the darkness. The tall man driving the coach wore a large black cape and a broad black hat. He pulled the powerful horses to a stop.

"You are early," the tall driver boomed at Jonathan's coachman.

"The English gentleman was in a hurry," the coachman replied nervously.

The tall man laughed, revealing sharp-looking teeth that glinted in the lamplight. "You can't fool me. You were trying to persuade him to go back with you. Bring me his luggage."

The coachman quickly retrieved Jonathan's luggage and tossed it into the carrier behind the seat of the tall man's carriage.

Jonathan scrambled out of the coach and scurried to the carriage. This two-seater was elegant, Jonathan observed, but no protection from the elements. And he'd have to share the seat with the driver.

The minute Jonathan leapt up onto the seat, the coach he'd been in turned abruptly. With astonishing speed, it vanished into the darkness. As Jonathan watched it leave, a strange chill came over him.

"I guess he was in a hurry to get home," Jonathan commented. The driver said nothing, but simply cracked his whip. The horses began a slow trot.

Jonathan squinted in the darkness to get a better look at the driver. But the high collared cloak and the wide-brimmed hat made it impossible for him to get a look at the guy's face.

"So," Jonathan began, "any four-star restaurants in the neighborhood? I couldn't find a single tourist guide."

The driver didn't respond.

Okay, thought Jonathan. This guy's not the talkative type.

A mournful howl broke the silence. Jonathan's fur stood on end. Wolves!

The sound was taken up by another, then another, till a wild howling began. It seemed to come from all over the county.

The horses snorted and strained at their bits. Jonathan could smell their fear.

The driver must have noticed Jonathan shivering. "There is a blanket under the seat," he offered in a thick accent.

Jonathan didn't want to admit it was fear and not cold that made him tremble. "Thanks," he said. He pulled the thick blanket over him with his teeth. After awhile, in spite of the strange circumstances, he grew drowsy. The rocking of the carriage and the late hour lulled Jonathan to sleep.

"Huh? Wazzat?" Jonathan woke with a start. He leapt to his paws and glanced around.

The carriage had stopped. *That must be what woke me*, he thought.

"Wait a sec," he said. "Where's the driver?"

Jonathan sat back on his haunches. Maybe he needed to make a rest stop, Jonathan realized. No bathroom on board makes this kind of travel a little inconvenient. I haven't seen any port-o-potty's or fire hydrants either. Luckily there are plenty of trees around.

Suddenly the horses began to snort and shriek. Jonathan clutched the reins in his teeth trying to control them. *What's wrong?* he wondered. He did not hear that awful howling anymore. *So what's spooking the horses?*

Jonathan's whiskers tingled. He smelled a rank and foul odor. Then the bright full moon sailed through the black clouds. It hovered low above the jagged crest of the cliffs.

Jonathan gasped. The wolves had stopped howling, but they circled the carriage. He was surrounded!

**Don't miss
my retelling of
Bram Stoker's Dracula
in . . .**

Scent of a Vampire